SKELETON CREW MANHUNT

Skeleton Crew Manhunt

Christopher Garraty

ARPress
45 Dan Road Suite 15
Canton MA 02021

Hotline:1(888) 821-0229
Fax:1(508) 545-7580

Ordering Information:
Quantity sales. Special discounts are available on quantity purchases by corporations, associations, and others. For details, contact the publisher at the address above.

Printed in the United States of America.

ISBN-13:   Paperback   979-8-89676-550-9
             eBook   979-8-89676-551-6
             Hardback   979-8-89676-552-3

Library of Congress Control Number: 2025920764

TABLE OF CONTENTS

DEDICATION

In memory of Brigantine, NJ Fire Chief James A. Holl, an exceptional public servant.

Memorial Mass

Greenlee, NJ

Church; just the thought of it filled him with a sense of dread. There were too many years of rigorous marching, kneeling and sitting and standing, getting jerked around by the arm by nuns and lay teachers. He disliked almost everything about it. The uncomfortable pews, the odd smell of the incense and the parade of people who came in, dressed up, good posture, an air of "better than thou" about them, some of them anyway. As a veteran police officer, Sergeant Morrow recognized most of them. Throughout the years he had seen many of them in their worst moments. A wife beater, a suspected child molester, thieves, drug addicts, liars and some people who just loved to spread gossip.

Herman Mitts hobbled in. Still showing the effects of having his leg broken by a baton, he had never forgiven Morrow for striking him. His mother had. Herman still refused to acknowledge him as he passed by. Mrs. Mitts would always nod and smile. Funny thing was, there were no more calls for family disturbances at the Mitts home. No more pushing his mother around, no more drunken rampages or verbal tirades. The only unfortunate habit he did not shake was his practice of spitting oyster sized hockers in a bucket of water he kept next to the living room sofa. The only reason he knew the spit bucket was still a part of the living room décor was a visit to the home for a small fire in the laundry room.

In the third row from the front was the Martin Larouse, owner of Filmore's diner. No telling what his involvement was a few years back when organized crime was pushing its way into town. At best he was an unknowing partner with gangsters, at the worst, a co-conspirator in the death of a police officer. Martin's Diner flourished after a tearful television interview with a national news reporter and his place became the unofficial command post for all of the television and print reporters that descended onto Greenlee during the Vincelli trial. It seemed like it all happened a few weeks ago at times. But now at the memorial mass marking the fifth anniversary of his friends' murder, he noticed how much had changed.

Dick Cambridge's wife arrived with her new gentleman friend, George. He was a pleasant fellow, nothing like Dick, but good to the kids. Dick's son Tim was noticeably taller and more mature looking. From time to time he stopped in the police station to soak up the atmosphere. It was apparent how much he had grown. His sister, as she grew was losing the memories of her father in spite of everyone's efforts to keep his memory alive. As Jean and the kids walked by she leaned into the pew and hugged Morrow and rubbed his back briefly. Did she know what he and the others had done for her? Most likely. Many suspected, no one really knew. As Jean and her family and Charles continued up the aisle, Tim reached over from behind and tapped Big John on his right shoulder and then stoically passed him on his left, then cracked a smile as John spotted him. No one else would get away with such childish behavior, but Big John had a soft spot for his late friend's children. John seemed to set aside his cantankerousness when it came to the Cambridge children.

It was strange seeing Big John in church. Morrow could only imagine what he was thinking while sitting there. Only he and Morrow really knew what happened the day Anthony Vincelli died at the court house. Well, except for Frank Duffield. Duffield was there but could probably pass a lie detector test if asked if he knew what actually happened to Vincelli. Duffield would never sit for a lie detector test. No of them would. None of them could really. Everyone had some sort of knowledge as to what happened, but only he and Big John actually knew. Well, maybe Sally. The pretty blonde waitress and mother of two sat directly in front of Morrow with her two sons. One was a recent college graduate, the other a sophomore now. The widow had successfully raised the two boys after her husband died suddenly when they were small. She worked around their schedules to make sure she was always home when they got home from school. If anyone knew what an important part she played in the events at the court house that day, the boys would have had a much different upbringing. As the other officers filled in the pews reserved for the police officers, Morrow began to feel a little more comfortable. Friends, acquaintances, co-workers and blood brothers like Big John and Bob Connolly were pulling it all together for Dick's family.

As their ranks grew, they played the "heathen or not" game. Watching the locals come into church and judging them by whether or not they would genuflect before entering the pew. A young couple carrying a baby in what appeared to be a plastic basket walked in and moved into a pew. A low murmur of "heathens," erupted from the group of officers.

Some parishioners sitting nearby turned and looked and began to smile as the officers continued.

A young woman wandered in and took a seat without dropping to one knee beforehand.

"Heathen," the group decried.

A frail man, probably in his nineties shuffled in using a cane and carrying his fedora grabbed the end of the pew and gave a slight nod to the crucifix on the wall in the front of the church. About eight of the forty officers now present declared "heathen."

"For Christ's sake, he's about two hundred years old. Cut him a break," Chief Wilson said shaking his head.

"Fuck 'im" a small group of officers murmured at the same time.

A stern looking elderly nun stopped next to the group and glared at what she thought were the offending officers. Morrow looked up at her and she at him. His heart skipped a beat.

"Move it along sister, nothing to see here," Big John said under his breath. After a brief pause and a sinister glare, the nun continued on.

Duffield walked by the officers and nodded as he passed. Of the several officers that were there, Duffield was more of a brother than most. Once gripped by the strong hand of alcoholism, Duffield had returned to form after beating the disease after encouragement from Dick Cambridge. Duffield dropped down to one knee, blessed himself and then rose and slid into a pew. A quick murmuring of self righteous sounding grumbling and some fake throat clearing from the officers elicited a few chuckles from the other attendees.

Then it started. Bag pipes. Nothing would bring a lump to the throat quicker than those damn bag pipes. Once he heard them the memories all came back. The flag draped coffin, the grieving widow, the crying children, the throngs of officers from near and far.

Morow remembered Dick coming to work during one of the hurricanes that passed through Greenlee. In his electric blue storm suit and police baseball cap, running from his car with his briefcase through high winds and rain, the briefcase popped open and the entire contents fell out and blew away before it could hit the ground. He turned and looked at the papers fly away in the storm and then continued running with his open briefcase for comedic effect.

"What was in there," Morrow had asked him.

"Only every scrap of paper that proves I am a cop," he said reaching into his rain jacket.

"I still got my badge though, that'll have to do."

"Where's my hat?"

"It blew off your head when the papers blew away."

"Lovely."

Morrow remembered the exchange like it was yesterday. Now, so many years later he fought back tears with the rest of the officers who each had their own stories of Officer Cambridge.

Morrow looked ahead and could see Sally pulling a tissue

out of her purse. Her youngest son put his arm around her. He could see her head drop while she was dabbing her eyes.

When the bag pipe music stopped the church was silent.

CHAPTER 1

THE COPS

Greenlee, New Jersey

Officer Doug O'Malley pulled his patrol car into the back of the police station on a warm Saturday morning. He couldn't wait to get out of it. Behind him in the back seat was a homeless man. The man was a stark contrast to the fit young officer with the crisp uniform and perfect haircut.

O'Malley pulled himself out of the car and pivoted on his heel and opened the back door for the stinking man. As he walked him into the rear entrance of the station, he knew his Sergeant would have something to say. Both men walked down the long hallway and turned into the operations room where Sergeant Morrow sat at his desk reading a newspaper. Sergeant Morrow glanced over his reading glasses and eyed the stinking man as he was directed toward the wooden bench.

"Need anything," the Sergeant asked.

"Nope. Just going to try to get him to the shelter."

Morrow looked the man over and with a quick glance noticed the man needed a new wardrobe, a shave, a bath and about fifteen thousand dollars worth of dental work. The man's teeth were mustard brown. No two teeth were going in the same direction. Some were rotten. As Morrow studied him, mischief brewed.

The man's outfit was a combination of dirty, well worn clothing from the late nineteen eighties. His powder blue fuzzy socks with the yellow crescent moon and star pattern made O'Malley wonder if a ten year old girl was still looking for them. Not only was the man homeless, he had been homeless for a long time. O'Malley knew Morrow didn't like bringing people into the station unless there was good reason to; too much liability. People fall, slip or sometimes antagonize officers and all hell breaks loose.

"I just have to call to see if they have any empty beds."

"Sure. That's fine."

O'Malley was surprised by the Sergeant's amiable demeanor.

"You want some coffee, Pop," Morrow asked the man.

"Sure," the man answered.

"Cream and sugar?"

"Yes. Please," the man said surprised that someone spoke as if he were a human being. It had been a long time since anyone really paid him any mind.

"Doug, you want anything?"

O'Malley looked up at his Sergeant suspiciously.

"Uh, no. Thank you though."

He watched as his Sergeant walked across the hallway to the coffee break room and opened the cabinet. O'Malley had worked with Morrow long enough to know something was up.

Suddenly, Morrow returned to the operations room with the holiest relic in the history of the Greenlee Police Department; a cream colored, ceramic mug with gold trim. It was the Chief's prized FBI Academy coffee mug; not really a mug, more of a chalice. The gold trim ran around the rim and down the handle. It sat on a pedestal base and had the official F.B.I. Training Academy crest on it. The Chief had worked hard for the honor of sipping coffee from it. The mug enabled him to discreetly let everyone one know he was an F.B.I. Academy graduate. Each day the Chief lovingly hand-washed it and then carefully placed the mug in the cabinet at quitting time. Morrow discarded the crumpled paper towel inside that had been used to dry it. It was a coffee mug of great importance, and Morrow handed it to the homeless man filled with piping hot coffee.

"Thanks, Sarge," the man said, taking his first sip.

O'Malley covered the mouthpiece on the phone

"The Rescue Mission has a bed open, I'll just take him... WHAT the...?"

"Listen, just to document that you were here, I have to take a photo of you, if that's o.k."

"No problem," the hobo replied.

Whipping out a digital camera from the sergeant's desk,

Morrow pointed it at him.

"Smile. Come on now, BIG smile."

The man smiled a big ugly yellow brown smile that showed how his teeth looked like a pile of pickup sticks.

"Hold the mug up a little higher."

CLICK.

"Got it. Thank you."

O'Malley dropped his head then lifted it to talk on the phone.

"We'll be there in a half hour or so. Thank you."

"God damn that's good coffee."

"Of course it is. What do you think we do in here all day," Morrow joked.

Officer Bob Connolly walked into the operations room. Bob was a fortyish, serious looking man, extremely nondescript. Of average height, weight and looks, he was famously forgettable, which came in quite handy when officers were being sued or subpoenaed. He immediately stopped and checked the bottoms of his shoes. Sergeant Morrow knew that Connolly was acting as if he thought he stepped in crap, but knew that Connolly knew, it was the odorous homeless man he smelled.

"Come on, we got you a spot in the Rescue Mission," O'Malley said, getting out of his chair. He waved the homeless man along with him.

"You can bring your coffee in the car."

Morrow shot out of his chair. O'Malley and the homeless man walked past Bob Connolly, and Connolly's face erupted into shock when he saw the Chief's coffee mug going out the back door, headed to the Rescue Mission.

"Wait until you see this," Morrow said handing Bob the digital camera.

Bob shook his head in amazement.

"There will be a federal investigation if that mug doesn't make it back."

"It wouldn't be our first," Morrow said as he sat down at his desk and went back to his newspaper.

Officer Ken Bogard walked in the rear door with a white paper bag. Morrow and Connolly looked up at him.

"Doughnuts?"

"Sorry Bob, muffins."

The young, handsome officer made his way to the sergeant's desk. Morrow snatched the bag and looked inside.

"These are all bran muffins."

Bogard snatched the bag from Morrow.

"That's all they had left. If you don't want any…"

"Let's not be hasty," Morrow backpedaled, taking a muffin from the bag.

The three men settled in behind their desks, enjoying muffins, coffee, and the newspaper. Morrow's eyes widened. He grabbed the sports section and left. Bob Connolly and

Ken Bogard shared an evil grin.

"We still have that golf club in lost and found," Connolly asked hopefully.

"Yes. Why?"

"Good, grab it. I got a surprise for the Sergeant," Connolly said, holding up a large firecracker.

"Holy shit! That's a half stick of dynamite," Bogard said while examining it closer.

"Nah, it's just an M-80."

"I don't know, it looks pretty big."

Both men moved to the hallway, just outside the men's room door. Connolly cracked the door open and saw a pair of black shoes and dark blue uniform pants in the stall. Connolly whispered.

"Just as I suspected, crapping!"

Connolly grabbed Bogard by the shoulders and positioned him perpendicular to the door and placed the golf club in his hands. Putting the explosive on the floor he lit it, opened the door and nodded to Bogard who dutifully launched it. As the door swung closed they could see the firework had landed in the sink. Inside, Deputy Chief Paul Moorehouse sat in the stall reading a golf magazine, pants around his ankles.

"Who's there?"

He could hear the door close. Outside the men's room Sergeant Morrow walked up on the unsuspecting Bogard and Connolly.

"What's going on?"

As Connolly saw Morrow behind him, he came to the sudden realization that the pants he saw under the men's room stall door did NOT have a yellow stripe on them thus indicating a Chief or Deputy Chief crapping, and not Sergeant Morrow.

"Let's go!"

The three officers scattered. Inside Deputy Chief Moorehouse strained to hear any more activity when the large firework exploded in the windowless, tiled rest room. His ears rang as bits of paper and a light smoke filled the room. Shards of the mirror were scattered everywhere. A black streak flew from the sink onto the tile wall, perhaps permanently. Dazed, Deputy Chief Moorehouse checked himself for gunshot wounds. Shaking his head, he grabbed his magazine and returned to reading.

CHAPTER 2

THE ROBBERS

Santee, California

Four armed men wearing lizard masks abruptly entered the First National bank of Santee. Barking orders, they took the staff and customers by surprise.

"Everybody on the floor! Do it now! On the floor!"

Several patrons dropped to the floor but some stood as if in shock. One patron, a heavy set man in his late twenties looked at the tallest of the robbers, his eyes squinting.

"Dude. You can't be serious. You want to rob a bank wearing a lizard mask?"

The robber pointed his rifle at him.

"On the ground now!"

The man looked down the barrel of the rifle.

"Is that even a real gun?"

The man reached for it but was interrupted by a punch to the side of the neck from another robber, knocking him to the floor. The rest of the patrons dropped to the floor except for one very pregnant woman. The second robber bent over and shouted in his face.

"Stay down. If you get up I'll show you this is real. Ya dig?"

"I dig," the man said covering his eyes with his fingertips like a child. A third robber whistled from the safe area.

"Let's go!"

The other two robbers gathered around the safe where two employees started loading money into the duffel bags. The tall robber moved to the front door noticing the driver sitting nonchalantly in the driver's seat. Two of the other robbers walked up behind him heavily laden with duffel bags.

"This is it. No more," one the robbers told him.

"Everybody look away," the tall robber barked. He pulled off his mask and slowly walked out of the bank, closing his grey trench coat over his rifle which was slung across his back and laid across his chest. He walked out, looked right, then left and nodded to the other three whom, as nonchalantly as they could, pulled off their masks and walked out of the bank carrying the loot. The driver popped the trunk. The others placed their bags inside. The tall robber got in the rear seat of the car, his heart now pounding.

"If the cops are onto us, this is when they'll get us."

He scanned the street as the others got in the car. The driver glanced in the rear view mirror.

"Everybody put your seat belts on," he said as he turned on his turn signal, checked the mirror and slowly pulled away from the curb.

"Holy shit! We did it! We robbed a bank!"

The other four men smiled and congratulated each other. It couldn't have gone any easier. Knowing that tellers were trained not to activate the hold-up alarm until after they left, the hardest part was staying calm and focused.

"I think fat boy was onto us," the muscular robber, Dave said.

"He knew our guns weren't real."

"He took it tough. I felt bad for him. I think he was a little slow," the tall robber said.

"But at least we can afford some real guns now."

The driver looked in the rear view mirror again checking for police.

"You guys are the lamest gang I ever worked for. Is this your first job?"

Dave leaned toward the driver.

"I've done plenty of stick ups before but never a bank. You know, we just held up a bank with guns that shoot plastic bb's and got away with it. I'd say that's pretty good."

The driver smiled as a drove slowly along the road.

"I have to hand it to you. No experience, no guns and wearing green lizard masks, and you STILL pull it off. Who got the masks? "

Everyone turned and looked at Dave.

"Hey. It was our first job."

"The next time," the driver said "get something a little more frightening, werewolf masks, the boogie man, Kim Kardashian, but no more lizards."

As their grey four door sedan cruised slowly onto the highway, two sheriffs' cars sped by in the opposite direction.

"Time to get off the street and split the loot," Dave announced.

THE CHIEF'S OFFICE

Greenlee, New Jersey

Chief Wilson sat in his office thumbing through his fishing magazine when Deputy Chief Paul Moorehouse knocked twice and strolled in.

"Hey Chief," Wilson said looking up at him.

"You gotta minute, Chief?"

"Always for you, what's on your mind? "

"An assassination attempt," Moorehouse said flatly.

Wilson tossed his magazine to the side and sat up straight behind his desk.

"Are you kidding me?" Wilson looked at him incredulously.

"I'm serious they tried to blow me up," the Deputy Chief complained. Captain Fertid walked in.

"Sorry Chief didn't know you were busy."

"No. Come in. Have a seat," Wilson told the Captain.

Captain Fertid shook hands with the elderly black man.

"The Deputy Chief was about to tell me who tried to kill him."

"Oh come on," Fertid said settling into a chair.

"Who'd want to kill you?"

"That's what I'd like to know."

The Deputy Chief put his hands out, palms up.

"Do I screw with anybody here? No. I sit in my office in City Hall, shuffle papers, flirt with all the ladies- who LOVE IT - I might add, and live and let live."

"What makes you think it was somebody here," Fertid asked.

"It happened right here, Saturday morning. In the men's room! While I was takin' a shit!"

Chief Wilson grimaced as the picture became clear.

"Why were you here on a Saturday morning," Wilson asked.

"I was going to Gus Oppenmueller's funeral. He lived in this city for almost eighty years. I thought I'd go and represent the city even though most of you probably haven't thought of him in years," Moorehouse intoned mildly chastising the Chief and Captain.

"I have to admit, I thought he died years ago," Wilson said with Fertid nodding in agreement.

"Well, anyway, I stop in to use the shoe shine kit in the O.I.C. desk, but it hits me. I gotta shit. So I'm in the men's room, shittin' and BOOM! Someone tried to assassinate me. I got paper and glass flyin' all around; my ears are ringing, smoke everywhere. Why are they fucking with me?"

"Who was in here when you came in," Fertid asked.

"No one. I didn't see a soul. But I never made it to the operations room."

"Who was working dayshift Saturday," Wilson asked the Captain.

Fertid sighed.

"Morrow, Connolly, Bogard, O'Malley. Tom Howard was dispatching. "

Wilson shook his head slowly.

"Captain, have Morrow see me in my office ASAP."

"I'm sure no one meant to assassinate you Chief."

Moorehouse grinned.

"I know. I'm just fuckin' with you. But they did make quite a mess."

"That's why I came in Chief. The mirror over the sink in the men's room is gone and there's a black streak in the sink and on the wall. Whatever it was, it was big. "

Moorehouse pulled himself out of the chair.

"Don't be too hard on him. We did much crazier shit than that and got away with it."

Wilson rolled his eyes slightly knowing Moorehouse was right. The Deputy Chief then put his hand out and flashed his most disarming smile.

"Maybe just put a little scare in them."

The Sergeant could hear the Deputy Chief's voice in the background when Captain Fertid called him on the radio:

"Sergeant Morrow, see me in the Chief's office." So did the others as they sat in their usual booth at Filmore's diner. Officer Bob Connolly's eyes widen as he smiled. Sally the waitress could read the men's reactions.

"Trouble," she asked. Bob Connolly nodded sheepishly.

"Received," Morrow answered on the radio knowing he would be grilled about the indoor fireworks once he got to the Chief's office. Then, as if an answer to his prayers, his radio came alive. Tom Howard's voice came over the air, calm, professional but a sense of urgency was evident from the first few syllables he broadcast:

"Unknown emergency at 134 9th street. Woman caller is hysterical, I'll start rescue."

Officer Ken Bogard jumped up from the table.

"I'll take it," he said taking one quick sip of his coffee before he left hurriedly.

"I'll head down too," Officer Connolly told Sergeant Morrow.

"Child drowning in the pool there!" Tom Howard's voice boomed over the radio.

"Paramedics notified and responding," he said as Morrow and Connolly darted from the restaurant. Sally watched the two men run to their cars. Jack Duffield looked at her.

"I don't envy them right now." Sally shook her head and started clearing their dishes. "I'll take their check," Duffield said pulling out a few bills. Sally placed it on the table in front of him.

In the pool 68 year old Martha Hamilton clung to the side, vomited in the water and tried in vain to push herself down into the bottom of the pool where her grandson lay. She could see his face, lifeless eyes staring out into nothing in particular. She could hear the sirens blocks away when suddenly a man in a suit broke through a section of the stockade fencing and jumped in the pool. Seconds later Officer Bogard ran in and jumped into the water. Morrow followed closely behind and reached for the exhausted, elderly woman. He noticed a cordless phone bobbing up and down on the top of the water. "Probably ruined," the Sergeant thought. Morrow could see it was Captain Fertid still in his suit and Bogard struggling to pull the boy's body from the drain cover on the bottom of the pool. Morrow took the woman by both arms and dragged her to the shallow end and let go when she began vomiting again. Bob Connolly arrived and threw the emergency shut off switch, turning off the vacuum from the pool's drain, releasing the boy's body.

Two firefighters arrived carrying a stretcher and backboard. Fertid and Bogard pushed the boy's body upward as the EMT's pulled the boy onto the concrete. One spoke into his radio.

"CPR in progress," and his partner folded the boy over,

watching water drain from him. Laying the body on the stretcher, one began checking for a pulse, the other sliding the C.P.R. board under the child. Trying to calm the hysterical woman, Morrow wrapped a towel around her while she screamed at the paramedics.

"Save him! Save him!"

Neighbors began peering through the gaping hole in the fence. Numerous radio transmissions squawked in the background on the police and fire channels. Captain Fertid climbed out of the pool and sat on the edge, taking deep breaths and watched as the young boy was wheeled out of the back yard toward the ambulance. Sergeant Morrow and Officer Connolly escorted the boy's grandmother. Chief Wilson walked into the back yard.

"Helicopter is on its way. It's landing at the baseball field." Fertid nodded, his suit stuck to him, hair askew and water puddled in his dress shoes. Wilson looked him over.

"You O.K.?"

Fertid reached into his jacket pocket and pulled out his cell phone.

"I am. My phone's not."

CHAPTER 4

IMAGE IS EVERYTHING

San Diego, California

As the bank robbers sat at the red light, a motorcyclist pulled alongside their car and slowly turned his head and looked them over. He was wearing a black leather vest, blue jeans worn beyond repair and large black motorcycle boots. He stopped and casually put his right foot down. He was wearing a face shield adorned with a fierce looking skull. The tallest robber, Richie looked back at him.

"Ho-lee shit! Look at that," he said to the rest of the robbery crew.

"That is what we need."

"Bad ass," the brown one they called "Mooj" said.

Richie rolled down his window.

"Hey, dude. Where'd you get that mask?"

The biker slowly turned his head and seemed to stare at him while his bike made a deep rumbling noise. The skeletal face seemed to be smiling at him, with a sinister sneer.

"Manuelo's Bike Shop in Santee. It's on Rosemont," the villainous looking biker offered.

"Thanks man. Pretty bad ass!"

The biker gave him the thumbs up and pulled away. The robbery crew pulled away slowly.

"If I was in a bank and four guys barged in wearing those masks, I'd shit myself," Carlos said.

Carlos was the newest and saltiest of the robbery crew. In his mid thirties, fit and good looking, he got by working as a bouncer in a few shady night clubs. It worked for him. An employee of a predominately cash business, no one really thought anything if he had wads of cash on him. He knew he had to be discreet when spending money. Level headed and smart, he planned on making a nice living robbing banks and retiring early. The rest of the gang laughed at his remark. They knew he wasn't easily scared.

"You guys got a few bucks now, right," Carlos said referring to the money they just brought in from their first robbery together.

"Let's take a trip to Manny's."

The others nodded in agreement.

"Richie is too tall," Carlos said.

"He'll stick out."

Richie felt relieved. He was the youngest of the robbers but possibly the smartest. Fresh out of high school, his childhood dreams of being a United States Marine were dashed when he found he was not physically able to qualify. A dream he nurtured for almost ten years had been dashed. He had no backup plan. He craved action but he was in no hurry to land on the radar of the local police department.

"Richie isn't even old enough to drive," Mooj said causing a few chuckles in the car. Richie shrugged his shoulders. Mooj wasn't far off.

As the car pulled into the parking lot of Manuelo's Bike Shop, the driver got out.

"Five masks. Anything else?"

CHAPTER 5

WEAPONS TRAINING

Oitmon, California

Deep in the desert Carlos and Mooj unloaded several folding tables and a canopy from the back of the pickup truck. Dave muscled four crudely made target holders with concrete bases about twenty five yards away and stopped when Carlos waived him off. Richie erected the canopy and put the four tables and five chairs underneath.

The driver pulled up in a four door Jeep and stopped behind the makeshift range. He watched the men setting up and noticed how each handled their tasks quietly and efficiently.

"Merry Christmas, boys!" he said smiling.

"Wait until you see the toys Santa has brought you."

Dave, Richie and Mooj gathered under the canopy. Carlos and the driver unloaded four Pelican cases off of the truck and placed them on the tables.

Opening the first one, the group saw a rifle. It *was* like Christmas morning. M-4 rifle, extra magazines, tricked out scope, sling, all black. Four of them packed nice and neatly in their own case.

"We're gonna have some fun with these," the driver said.

"What's in the other cases?"

"Mooj, that is a case of MP-5's, full auto. That's what we're gonna play with tomorrow, as long as no one shoots themselves today."

The driver was a mystery to Richie, Dave and Mooj. It was obvious that he and Carlos had worked together for a while and he usually seemed serious. Playing with guns undoubtedly excited him. Carlos had really pulled the group together but the driver seemed to have the connections. Inside information on banks, connections to people who could make authentic false identifications and resources to put together a small training camp in the desert. He was an inspiration to the young and inexperienced bank robbers. He impressed upon them that this job they had was like any other. They were expected to come to work sober, clean and well rested.

He impressed upon them that even if they were arrested for a minor violation, depending on the circumstances, each one could go to jail, depending on their past criminal history. As such, the driver explained to them the procedure they had to guard each man's share while he was incarcerated. They did this out of fairness and to diminish the temptation to rat out the other members of the crew. It was a well run company even if it was highly criminal. The driver was clearly an administrator in addition to being a fine getaway driver. Carlos was the first line supervisor. He was knowledgeable, a good instructor and instilled in the men a sense of loyalty to himself and each other. He was molding them into a team.

CHAPTER 6

THE SHOE IN

Greenlee, New Jersey

Marshal Frost sat in the art gallery looking at a long thin painting. His white hair contrasted his dark blue suit. He was a dapper man. From time to time he'd strike a pose right out of a nineteen seventies cigarette commercial. He wouldn't be seen without his highly polished shoes and large wristwatch. A small pinky ring adorned his right hand and he always smelled like a fresh haircut. Skilled in the fine art of schmoozing and posing, Frost could talk most people into a lot of things. Unless you did your homework and found that most of what he was telling you was self-serving and false, you'd feel grateful that he included you in his plans, whatever they were at the moment.

Dark and mysterious, the painting hung by itself with a small bench directly in front of it. As Frost settled on the bench, he looked at the painting and wondered why he liked it.

"Francois Dupah," he read on the small brass plate underneath.

"Francois must have had some mental problems," Frost decided.

As he studied it he could hear footsteps coming up behind him.

"Right on time," Frost thought as he turned to see Detective Leoni offer his hand. Leoni was handsome, fit, polished and eager. Frost shook his hand, almost as an afterthought.

"Have a seat," he said to Leoni, sitting back and waiting for the heaps of thanks and praise he was due.

"So, how are things in the detective bureau?"

Leoni smiled.

"Great. Those midnight shifts were killing me. It is nice being out of patrol."

"I told you I'd take care of you."

"Yes you did," Leoni said, acknowledging Frosts power. He had kept his promise to have the young patrolman moved to the dick bureau.

"I just couldn't see a young man of your skill and intellect breaking up bars fights and shaking door knobs on the midnight shift. Your talents will be put to much better use as a detective."

Leoni swelled with pride.

"It is just so much easier going to school while working a steady shift, and my wife loves that I am home in time for dinner. I really can't thank you enough."

Frost drew a deep breath and sat back on the bench and carelessly adjusted his tie.

"I'm glad you said that," Frost said lowering his voice and leaning a bit closer to Leoni.

"I know a way you can repay me."

"Name it," Leoni said, regretting that he sounded so eager.

"I'd like you to keep an eye on things, let me know what's going on within the department, the mood of the men, the rumors, just like you used to do for Councilman Papadopoulos. Now that he is in prison, we need to keep things running smoothly, like before, but now I want you to keep *me* in the loop."

"I understand," Leoni said avoiding eye contact, knowing that Frost was looking directly at him.

"There is one more thing," Frost told the detective.

"We're having the City Manager post a promotional exam notice."

Leoni nodded.

"You don't seem excited," Frost said.

"It doesn't affect me. I won't be eligible for two more years."

"Well," Frost paused for dramatic effect, "we decided to review the promotional procedures and dropped the requirement from five years to three years."

"So I'll be eligible in about three weeks? That's kind of sudden."

"Does that mean you aren't interested?"

"Oh no, I'm interested, but the other guys, well, they'll chide me I am sure."

"Fuck 'em. You're going to have to build that wall between you and your subordinates anyway, might as well start now."

Leoni looked at Frost. Knowing he could make it happen he sat up straight looked Frost directly in the eye and shook his hand.

"I guarantee you I will come out number one in the written phase of testing."

"That's what I like to see! Confidence!"

"I am looking forward to the challenge," Leoni told him.

"Just remember our agreement. You are my eyes and ears in the department. I have big plans for you."

Outside the art gallery Detective Leoni opened his unmarked police car and climbed in. He could see Councilman Frost getting in his station wagon on the other side of the lot. Leoni wondered if he could believe his promises. Looking around at his detective car and the detective badge on his belt, the young detective decided that he could.

Leoni considered that he'd have to walk a tight rope. Not enough information and he'd piss off Frost possibly upsetting the deal, too much sensitive information and he could be headed for the same fate as Councilman Gregor Papadopoulos and his nephew Theo. Gregor Papadopoulos was now serving a seven year sentence. Theo, having escaped criminal charges, landed on the wrong end of an internal affairs investigation that saw him demoted and assigned to the midnight to eight shift. Leoni suddenly realized he hadn't actually laid eyes on Theo for months, nor had he seen anything with his name on it come through the detective bureau. It was as if he wasn't there at all.

"Probably a good person to stay away from anyway," he thought. "Or, possibly a good person to get to know a little better and maybe pick up the finer points of intelligence gathering for the politicians."

Leoni watched Frost pull out and decided to wait a few minutes before he left too. No sense in advertising the connection to Marshal Frost. The fewer who knew, the better.

CHAPTER 7

PROMOTION NOTICE!

Greenlee Police Station

Inside the operations room of the Greenlee Police Station, Sergeant Morrow listened intently to the woman on the other end of the telephone and nodded politely.

"Yes ma'am. I understand. We can send an officer down to perform an exorcism."

Connolly threw his head back and began shaking it back and forth.

"I am not going. I will not go!" he whispered.

Morrow held up his index finger at Connolly.

"Yes ma'am. He *is* a fine officer. He is right in front of me and he'd be more than happy to come down… It's no trouble at all. We'll see you soon."

"Don't tell me, let me guess," Bob complained.

"The little men are throwing white powder in her face

again," Morrow interrupted.

"I'm not going," Connolly told Sergeant Morrow.

Captain Fertid walked in carrying a piece of paper and tacked it to the bulletin board. He looked at Morrow and shook his head slightly and walked out of the room.

"He looks pissed," Connolly said taking the paper off of the board.

Patrolman Ken Bogard walked in saw Morrow and Connolly pouring over the notice.

"Promotional exams," Morrow said scanning the document.

"Three years in service, they dropped it from five years" Connolly said. He continued reading the announcement.

"Associates degree preferred. Preferred? That means they've opened it up to people without a degree," Morrow observed.

"Who has less than five years and doesn't have their associates' degree?"

"Five officers have less than five years. Only one doesn't have his degree yet. Detective Leoni," Morrow deduced.

Bogard was puzzled.

"Leoni?"

"They've tailored the test requirements to allow Leoni to be eligible. Of all of the candidates, he is the only one affected by both of the changes," Morrow told him.

"So you can tell who is going to be promoted just by the criteria of the test?"

"It's a damn shame, isn't it?"

Connolly grabbed his portable radio and clipped it on his belt.

"I have to go perform an exorcism…again!"

"Just check on her and make sure she's o.k." Morrow added.

"Alright" Connolly said heading for the door.

"Unless there really are little men throwing powder in her face."

"I'll call you if that's the case" Connolly said as he rounded the corner.

CHAPTER 8

SHOOT HOUSE!

Beaver Trap, California

Carlos arrived with four men dressed in black BDU's; serious looking men. They were fit, weathered and each was in their forties. As they climbed out of the SUV they unloaded their gear from the back of the truck.

Carlos gestured toward the shoot house. A wooden structure with a tarpaulin roof, it stood alone in the woods. The doorways were covered with overlapping eight inch strips of heavy clear plastic. The four men nodded to Richie, Mooj and Dave and went inside without a word.

The house was located on the far side of a several acre piece of land, half of which was a paint ball facility. The shoot house was reserved for serious paint ball players, law enforcement, military and other professionals who didn't want to mix with the teenagers and novices.

Carlos tossed each of his men a black duffel bag filled with black Velcro laden protective gear. He set up a folding table outside the main door and laid out a variety of paint ball guns.

"This is going to be fun," Richie said looking over the guns.

Carlos watched as Mooj held the large black protective cup upside down and placed it over his nose. He looked at the long straps. Puzzled, he asked "Does this snap into the helmet?"

"Actually, these straps go round your waist and the cup goes over your grommets," Carlos told him.

As Dave, Richie and Mooj wrestled into their vests and cups, Carlos assisted with the neck protection, helmet and charging the paint ball guns. He checked his own gear ensuring full coverage.

"This isn't a video game, if you get hit it'll sting," Carlos warned.

As the men adjusted their helmets and face masks, Carlos knew it was coming. The black masks coupled with the black helmet gave an impression of a famous sci-fi villain. Someone would say it...any second now.

"Luke. I am your father. Come to the dark side. Kaaaaaawwww, koooooooo," Richie said accentuating his impersonation with the mechanical breathing sound.

Dave and Mooj were just as anxious to start as Richie. They looked at each other through the masks on the helmets. A black glove emerged through the heavy plastic strips and gave a thumb up.

"O.K. one at a time you're going to walk through the shoot house and clear the rooms. The boogie men will be waiting for you and if you see them and they are armed, shoot them. If they aren't, don't shoot them. It's as easy as that. It starts at the first whistle; scenario is over after the second whistle. Keep all of your gear on until you are back outside and I tell you to take it off." Everybody nodded in agreement.

The whistle was heard. Carlos nodded to Mooj. Holding his paint ball rifle close and high, he burst through the doorway. Richie and Dave stood outside with Carlos. Their hearts were pumping. They could hear Mooj kicking doors open.

"Pop pop," they heard indicating his first encounter. A blood curdling scream was heard and another four shots were heard, then laughter.

"Startle effect, we'll go over that," Carlos told them.

Again they heard Mooj making his way around the rustic wooden structure. As he made his way around plastic furniture and rubber mannequins, the others listened to the paint ball war going on inside. Carlos could hear paintballs hitting various items, hollow plastic furniture, wooden walls and plastic face shields.

After a short whistle blast the four men in black came out along with Mooj.

"Everybody put your guns on the table! You can remove your face shield."

The leader of the black clad men approached Carlos. He

was about five foot seven and had graying hair. He looked like he could have been a retired policeman.

"Tactically he's good. He moves well. We got him good with the person hiding in the closet."

Mooj shook his head sheepishly.

"Yeah, you got me. Whoever the screamer was, they scared the living shit out of me."

Carlos turned to Richie and Dave.

"Startle effect, when something scares you so bad you fire. That's why you keep your finger off the trigger until you are ready to fire."

"He looked good otherwise, his shots were on target. He checked all of his dead spaces."

"Thanks Chris," Carlos said. The instructor nodded and grabbed his helmet and signaled for his group to go back inside.

"Richie you're up," Carlos told him.

The whistle blasted. Richie had a sudden surge of adrenalin and entered the structure like he was on fire.

"Pop! Pop!" was heard almost immediately.

"Get on the ground! Get on the ground!"

Outside, Dave imagined Richie came across the unarmed person.

Several volleys of shots were heard and then it stopped.

"Sounds like Richie got 'em all."

Carlos shrugged his shoulders. A moment went by and one single pop was heard. The whistle blew. Richie and the four men in black came out.

"What happened," Carlos asked.

"The unarmed man I made get on the ground got up after I left the room. He picked up one of the dead guys rifles and snuck up behind me."

"Other than that you were perfect. He did everything the right way. Multiple shots on each target, checked his dead spaces, held his gun close when he opened the closet door. He looked good."

"Back in," the leader told his minions.

Dave prepared to go inside. Carlos adjusted his neck protector and tucked it into his vest. The whistle blew.

"Where's your cup," Carlos asked as Dave entered.

As Dave passed through the plastic strips the men could see him bending over trying to see his protective cup through his face shield.

The first few moments were quiet. Mooj, Carlos and Richie stood outside and heard several shots, after a few seconds, several more. The whistle blew.

The four men in black emerged and Dave followed. He was covered with day glow orange, pink, blue and green paintball hits all over the front of his vest and mask.

"Jesus! You look like a clown threw up on you! What happened," Richie asked.

"I walked in a room and saw someone hiding behind the sofa. I rushed in and didn't see someone hiding behind the door. It was a blood bath!"

"What's the lesson here," the lead role players asked.

"Don't rush in. Check for multiple shooters."

"Excellent. Let's do it again."

CHAPTER 9

DID 'JA EVER NOTICE...?

Greenlee Police Detective Bureau

Detective Leoni peered at his laptop screen trying to focus on the important lessons at hand: "Compare and contrast the rates of decomposition of a human body buried in a shallow grave in the American Southwest and the Upper Central states region. Give examples of variations of rates by season."

"Got to move onto something easier for starters," he decided. Flipping through the chapter review; he stopped to read:

"Give examples of the similarities of the physical characteristics of the native people of Southern Asia and Native Americans. What are differences?"

Bob Connolly walked into the detective bureau and saw Detective Leoni sitting at his desk reading.

"Hey," Connolly barked, startling the Detective.

"What's up," Leoni asked as he sat back in his chair. He

minimized his screen so no one would know he was studying for the sergeants' exam on city time.

"My wife is interested in taking ballroom dancing lessons. I thought I'd see if you could give me any insight into the whole thing."

"Sure. What do you want to know?

Connolly sat on the edge of the desk and pretended to search for a question.

"What kind of shape do you have to be in? I know I'm a little bit older than you."

"We took lessons for quite a while but we weren't in it for competition like some people are. To be honest with you I was a bit winded when I first started but it is so much fun you get in shape pretty quickly."

"I see. I'm not real keen on it but my wife is, so you know how that goes."

"I do. If momma ain't happy, no one is happy. If you want," Leoni continued, "I'll call you the next time we go out dancing. You can meet us."

Connolly appeared to consider the offer.

"Sure. I'll let the missus know. That would be great. I'd like to see what I might be getting myself into."

Captain Fertid stormed into the office obviously perturbed.

"Is your radio on?"

Leoni picked up his portable radio and turned it on.

Fertid looked at him with disdain.

"There's another burglary on Sheridan Place. Go down there and help the district car."

Leoni closed the laptop and opened his top desk drawer and took his semi automatic pistol out. He placed it in his holster and snapped it closed as Connolly and Fertid watched. Afterward the Detective nervously grabbed his notebook and radio.

"Keep your radio on," Fertid reminded him.

"Yes sir," Leoni said scurrying out of the room.

Bob Connolly watched him leave and looked at the Captain.

"What the hell are you doing here? Hit the street, we have a burglar to catch."

Connolly smiled and slid off of the desk and left. Fertid stood there watching him, shaking his head.

"Fucking guys around here," he thought.

CHAPTER 10

ROLL CALL!

Greenlee Police Station

Sergeant Morrow entered the roll call room and could feel the buzz. Officers were excited about the new criteria for the promotional exams and every officer had his own theory on how things would go. Most of the seasoned officers could see that both changes on the criteria were tailored for Detective Leoni. As Morrow took the podium, the talking continued. As he looked around the room he saw Big John sitting in the back row. John saw Morrow and shrugged his shoulders.

"O.K.! Listen up!"

The talking wound down and Morrow continued.

"First item, we are getting hammered with burglaries on the midnight shift. We had three reported yesterday and three more today. Keep an eye out for anyone suspicious and let the detectives know if you find anything out of the ordinary."

"Glory hounds," emanated meekly from the group of about a dozen officers.

Most of the officers were content to nod their heads and make mental notes. Big John raised his hand.

"What are they taking?"

"Booze, food, a couple of cameras, some jewelry and silver items like silverware, candle stick holders."

"Times," Big John asked.

"We're not sure since some of the homes are empty but it seems like late at night or early in the morning for the others."

Big John nodded and flashed his most sarcastic smile and rolled his eyes.

"Item two. If you haven't heard, the new criteria for the sergeants' test is posted. If you are interested, please submit your letter to the Chief."

Big John raised his hand.

Morrow knew what was coming. By virtue of his rank, Big John was going to force Morrow to defend the testing policy changes.

"John?"

"Sarge, everyone knows Detective Leoni has an in. Why bother?"

"Well, even if that were true, why wouldn't you?"

"Why would you," Big John immediately countered.

Morrow drew in a breath as he thought.

"Well, for starters, suppose Leoni does have an in. I'm not saying he does, but just for the sake of argument. Suppose he can't take a test?"

Big John rolled his eyes, obviously disappointed in the answer.

"Suppose Leoni accidently shoots someone on the range? How about if he murders his wife in a fit of rage? Where would you be? Ineligible because you didn't take the test."

"I see your point," Big John relented.

"Things are not always as they seem," Morrow said.

Connolly turned around and looked at Big John and smiled. John casually flipped the bird to Connolly and whoever else was looking.

"One other thing; check the range schedule. If you are scheduled to go while you are working please come back in a timely fashion. We don't want to leave our brother officers short on the street, do we?"

"Oh no," emanated from the crowd of officers, oozing with sarcasm.

"O.K. Hit the street. Go find that burglar. Stay safe and put your seatbelts on!"

As the officers filed out the back door Connolly approached Morrow.

"Who are you? Braveheart?"

Morrow smiled and patted him on the back.

"You have to give them hope, even if it is a false hope."

"Funny you should mention that," Connolly said smiling.

CHAPTER II

STEPPING IT UP

San Francisco, California

Richie put on his protective gear, tactical vest and slung his new M-4 rifle over his shoulder letting it lay across his chest. He placed his grey trench coat over it and buttoned it as well as he could.

"Bulky, but not entirely noticeable."

"This will change everything," he thought placing the skeleton mask on his face and turning to the mirror in his hotel room. It was an impressive sight. Richie stood six feet six inches, sometimes he was measured at six foot seven, but being so tall it was hard for shorter people to accurately measure him. He looked at the trench coat and adjusted his gear underneath to make it smoother. Ballistic cup, ceramic plate in his vest, shin guards, gloves, ammo, quick ties, pepper spray. He looked himself over and double checked that he had everything. He made sure his weapon was safe. Today it would be another bank. As planned, the driver would call in a false call across town to get the local police moving in the

occurred approximately thirty five minutes ago. White male driver, no other information."

Officer Geeman shined his flashlight on the green Plymouth as O'Malley stuffed the drunk driver in the back of his car.

"Officer O'Malley has the vehicle here, and the driver is in custody." O'Malley looked at Geeman who was still examining the car.

"We have long, auburn hair and blood on the front of the car, in the grill and on the driver's side headlight."

O'Malley was shocked but decided to play it cool.

"How the hell did you see that at night," Geeman asked. O'Malley just smiled and pretended he knew all along.

CHAPTER 13

THAT SINKING FEELING

Officer Bob Connolly climbed the stairs to the detective bureau and entered Leoni's office. Again, Leoni minimized the screen on his computer so as not to get caught studying on duty.

"Hey, I'm glad you stopped by. My wife and I had a great time dancing last night. It's a shame you couldn't make it."

Connolly sat on the edge of Leoni's desk.

"Yeah, I asked my wife but she wasn't up for it, but she is still interested."

"Good. I can't wait to see you two in action."

Connolly switched gears.

"How about that sergeant's exam? I've been looking over the material and it doesn't look like much of it applies to us."

"I know. I just read the chapter on statistics and thought we are such a small department; we can do the statistics in our heads. It really is a waste of time."

Captain Fertid burst into the office.

"Is your radio on?"

Leoni turned the button on the top and an audible "click" was heard.

"Fuck," he said, frustrated with himself.

"Why are you two sitting in here bitching about the sergeants' exam and not on the street finding this burglar?"

"Well, um," was all Leoni could muster.

Fertid continued.

"A district car is out at 208 Vernon Place on another burglary. Get down there and dust for prints or something! You aren't going to catch any criminals in here."

Leoni shot out of his chair and opened his desk drawer, which was empty. A look of dead came over his face.

"What is wrong," Captain Fertid barked.

"My, uh, gun, I must have left it in my briefcase after going to the range," Leoni said his eyes darting back and forth. Connolly watched the reaction on Captain Fertid's face which was a mixture of incredulity and disdain.

"Are you sure?" Fertid asked him.

"Oh yes," Leoni said panicking.

"I'll run down and get it out of the car. I'm sure it's in the trunk," Leoni told his captain.

"I'll head down to the area and interview some neighbors," Connolly said as he walked out. Once in the hallway he broke out into a broad grin. Officer O'Malley looked at him suspiciously as they passed each other in the hallway.

"O'Malley," Fertid called.

"The Chief wants to see you."

O'Malley headed into the office with Fertid close behind. Despite the fact he had been up all night and halfway through the morning working on the fatal drunk driving arrest, O'Malley was not the least bit tired. He had a spring in his step as he walked in.

"Hey! It's the man of the hour," the Chief said shaking his hand. Fertid stood off to the side with his hands in his pockets.

"I just wanted to congratulate you on a nice bust."

"Thanks Chief," O'Malley said, "but I have to be honest. I had no idea he had just killed someone, I noticed he had a dim headlight."

The Chief asked "*Then* what did you do?"

"I pulled him over."

"Exactly. How many prima donnas would have just driven by and thought nothing of it. We've got guys who think stopping cars is beneath them. You saw something and you looked into it. That's how shit gets done. Don't sell yourself short. Just think about what those officers standing in the road over that poor lady's carcass thought when they got the word you caught the guy."

O'Malley hadn't thought it out that far.

"Probably saved them a lot of paperwork."

Fertid stepped forward and put his hand on O'Malley's shoulder.

"A lot of stress too. The case is solved. All they have to do is document what happened."

"You make all of us look good when you guys make an arrest like that. You really do."

"Thanks, Chief, Captain," O'Malley stood up and headed out of the office when Detective Leoni passed him walking in.

"Keep up the good work," the Chief said as O'Malley left.

Detective Leoni's heart sank.

"What can I do for you detective?"

"Chief, I think someone has stolen my gun".

Fertid looked at him but Leoni couldn't look back.

CHAPTER 14

INTERNAL AFFAIRS STATEMENT

Greenlee Police Department

"So let me get this straight," the Chief said. "You went to the range yesterday, came home and cleaned your gun. This morning, you put it in your desk drawer when you got to work, and now it is missing."

"Yes sir," Leoni said steadfastly.

"Did you go anywhere last night?" Fertid chimed in.

"Yes. My wife and I went to the Circus Tavern."

"Did you take your gun with you?"

"No sir. I never take my gun with me when I go out drinking."

"I see," the Chief said. The tone in his voice suggested he was not convinced.

"But this morning you told the Captain that it was in your briefcase in the trunk of your car."

"I did sir, but when it was missing I just assumed…"

Fertid held his hand up.

"What made you say it was in your briefcase?"

"That's where I put it on the way home from the range."

"But you said you took it home and cleaned it," the Chief countered.

"I did, and this morning I brought it to work with me."

"You're sure?"

"Yes, I remember smelling it on the way here, the gun cleaning solution."

The Chief let out a sigh.

"What did you have to drink last night?"

"Two martinis."

The Chiefs eyes darted to Captain Fertid, obviously looking for his reaction to the Detective drinking a less manly drink than beer or whiskey.

"Two martinis, huh?"

"Captain Fertid, I think we have to assume someone stole his gun."

Fertid nodded.

"Of course you realize leaving a loaded gun in an unlocked desk drawer is in violation of our department's rules and regulations."

"I do," Leoni admitted as his heart pounded and a sour surge erupted in his stomach.

"Any idea of who it might be," the Chief asked.

"Not really. I don't know who would want to screw with me."

"You have to be the stupidest person in the world if you don't," the Captain thought.

"We'll start an Internal Affairs file. I'll put Detective Fritz on it."

CHAPTER 15

AGENT DONOVAN F.B.I.

Anthony Donovan walked briskly toward his supervisor's office. He knocked on the office door frame. Edwin Brimley waved him in. Brimley directed Donovan toward a chair with a quick sweeping motion. Another agent was standing, leaning forward and holding on to the back of another chair. He was overweight and wore glasses that were frosted at the top. Donovan knew of him.

"This is recent transferee, Anthony Donovan."

The heavy set man turned and offered his hand.

"It's nice to meet you Mister Tizol. I'm a big fan of Operation Dog and Pony," Donovan offered respectfully.

"Thanks kid."

Donovan didn't like being referred to as "kid".

"A kid is a baby goat," he thought as he smiled politely.

"How do you like California?" Tizol asked.

"Well, it's exactly as described," Donovan said being purposely non committal.

Tizol pushed his bulk up off the back of the chair and took a deep breath, poked his finger down the front of his shirt collar and ran it around, twisting his head trying to get more air.

"I'll check in with you later," Tizol said dismissively to Brimley, unaware of the disdainful look Brimley shot him.

"See ya kid," Tizol bellowed to Donovan as he walked out huffing and puffing.

"That's out superstar," Brimley said.

"He spent a lot of years undercover," Donovan retorted.

"Probably that persona takes root after a while."

"I can't say I like it."

"Not standard BU issue," Donovan agreed.

Brimley closed one large file and opened another.

"What do we have so far?" Brimley asked quickly.

"Not a whole lot, but I think this half ass lizard masked robbery gang may have graduated to using real guns," he told his boss.

"I know I got this case because it is a laugher, but there are some similarities with them and two other bank robberies that happened shortly afterward in Northern California."

"How so," Brimley asked sitting back in his chair looking up at the ceiling waiting to be convinced.

"The crew with the pellet guns, *if* they were pellet guns, had three guys we know of, most prominently a tall thin guy about six foot five, two averaged sized guys, one maybe Middle Eastern and a white driver. All three robberies had an exceptionally tall white guy, we know the one in Sacramento had a guy with dark skin, maybe Hispanic."

"Tall guy, brown guy," Brimley repeated back.

"Thus far this crew has failed to unmask themselves in front of witnesses or video cameras," Donovan stated plainly.

"Probably not likely," Brimley added.

"Agreed," Donovan said raising his finger.

"However, multiple witnesses agree that at least two of the suspects appear to have tactical training. Others think they might be athletes of some sort. They seem to be very agile, very familiar with their weapons."

"So, they work out. You think they might be military?"

"Military, cops, paintballers, maybe video gamers."

"Video gamers?"

Donovan nodded.

"Many of the video games out there have detailed information on weapons, tactics, jargon; you can play online against people from all over the world. An eighth grader in the States might be playing some shoot 'em up game against some Marine in Afghanistan, provided he had internet access."

Brimley looked at Donovan suspiciously.

"You've never played video games, have you?"

"Pacman, Tetris, is this the type of stuff you're talking about?"

"Not really sir."

Brimley sat up in his chair.

"What I'd like to do is consolidate these three robberies and treat them as one group. Obviously the second and third are connected."

"How so?"

"In both of those robberies all of the gunmen were wearing skeleton face shields, the face shields motorcyclists wear. It's in my report."

"Yes. But from what I read, the lizard masked bandits seemed like they were not experienced, or they were sort of lame."

"I wonder if they picked up someone else," Donovan offered.

"How about if we change their designation from the lizard gang to the Skeleton Crew?"

Brimley smiled.

"OK, let me know what you need."

"Thank you, sir," Donovan said rising from his chair.

"I'm going to look into this video game combat stuff, it sounds like it is really taking off, huh?"

"Yes sir. It just might."

CHAPTER 16

SITUATIONAL AWARENESS

Fresno, California

The driver picked them up as arranged at the parking lot of an abandoned department store. Richie climbed into the minivan with his rifle slung over his shoulder, followed by Dave. Carlos climbed in the rear seat while Mooj sat up front with the driver. Carlos handed a bundle for Richie to pass up to the driver, which he did.

"It's your share from the last job."

The driver pretended to judge the weight by holding it up in his hand and moving it up and down.

"Cool."

As the van rolled out of the parking lot Carlos spoke up.

"Dave and Mooj, contact. Richie, watch for the tellers trying to pull the alarm. I'll cover. I'm going to move to the right, take the corner and cover from there."

The men nodded having gotten comfortable in their roles

from their previous robberies.

"Anything goes wrong, what do we do Richie?"

"Get the fuck out."

"The alarm gets pulled?"

"Get out."

"A teller gets feisty or loud?"

"Get out."

"A fat lady drops dead of a heart attack?"

"Adios muchachos."

"Why?"

"Because if anyone dies while we're there, the felony murder act kicks in. We're all charged with murder."

"Correct," Carlos told him pulling out a plastic bucket.

"Cell phones and wallets."

The men tossed their belongings in.

"We're in, we're out. No fuss. No muss. No one gets hurt. We get rich. Maybe we'll hit a nice steak house tonight."

"Sounds good to me," Mooj said as he checked his M-4 making sure he had one in the chamber. Richie checked his weapon and checked his magazine pouch to make sure the rounds were facing in the right direction.

"How about you driver?" Carlos asked.

"Working another job. Sorry. I appreciate the offer," he

said.

It was the first time Richie had heard Carlos speak so casually to the driver in front of the other men. He was a quiet man and seemed to have been coached beforehand by Carlos. He would pick up the crew, drive to the job, wait and get them out in a hurry and drop them off to an awaiting car or truck. Obviously he knew Carlos but they seemed to act as if they didn't. Richie wondered why.

As the team headed to the bank, Richie pictured where he'd position himself. He had gone inside the bank prior to the robbery. Dave went in to buy a money order. Mooj went in to get a nice crisp fifty dollar bill for a birthday card. Carlos went in to ask for directions. Richie went in to cash in a jar of change at the automated coin counter. Each one went in on a different day and reported back with their impression of staffing, layout and an overall competence of the employees inside. There were no guards. Of the banks they had robbed, Richie felt this was going to be an easy target since it was such a densely populated area with numerous parking garages.

Michelle Fedemah stood behind the counter and squeezed more hand sanitizer on her hands and rubbed them dry. Her feet hurt and as a result, her back hurt as did her hips. She hated when contractors and landscapers came in with a lot of cash. Getting in line with the rest of the customers they sparked fury when others who might be off on their lunch break or under some other time constraints would moan when these men plopped the cash on her counter with a deposit slip.

"Isn't there someone else who can do that? In an office perhaps?"

She usually smiled when they groused. She would count the cash as fast as she could. But as fast as she could go, she felt the pressure. The others weren't any help either. Roger, the overweight, self righteous ninny would put up his "next window please" sign as soon as he saw them enter the bank. He did it every time. It wasn't that he was lazy, although he was; he just enjoyed sticking it to her.

Roger snapped into action as soon as he saw the masked men enter the bank. Placing the "next window please" sign on the counter he turned quickly.

"Not so fast, fat ass," he heard.

Michelle looked at him and he froze. The first robber drew a rifle out of his trench coat and backed into a corner yelling.

"Everybody get on the ground. Now!"

His movements were such that she knew he was experienced. The authority in his voice, the fluidity of his movements terrified her. Two other men dressed similarly rushed in. The muscular one grabbed Roger by the throat.

"You have twenty seconds to get that safe open," Roger squealed like a pig. His hands flew up and he shook them back and forth overcome by fear. The tall robber pointed at Michelle.

"You! Empty all the cash drawers in the bag."

He tossed a black nylon duffel bag at her. The man in the corner scanned the room with his rifle.

"Nobody move! Stay on the floor!"

It was obvious to her no one wanted to move. A dozen or so patrons were now lying on the floor motionless. As Michelle placed the cash in the bag, the tall robber whispered to her.

"Take it easy, we'll be out of here in a minute. No one is going to get hurt."

He moved like the man in the corner. He had a sense of purpose, athleticism and determination but he was calmer, more relaxed than the others. Then she noticed Larry. Larry worked as an armed guard at the jewelry store down the street. As he walked in the front door, he was texting.

"Oh my God," Michelle said as the masked man in front of her turned toward the guard. The guard instinctively drew his pistol in a smooth, seemingly effortless motion. Michelle watched as the robber in front of her started to crouch but stopped.

"Don't do it," the guard yelled as he moved toward Michelle and the tall robber.

"Get on the floor," Larry yelled at the masked man. Larry had the drop on him.

It was as if someone had flung something in her face as hard as they could from a few inches away. It stung and something had entered the corner of her eye causing her to flinch and double over.

She popped back up from behind the counter and saw the robber with his back to her and the gunman in the corner moving out into the middle of the floor.

"Let's go. We're done," he yelled. Larry lay on the floor

with much of the top half of his head gone or turned inside out. Blood and brain had sprayed across her counter, her clothing, the money, the bag and the wall behind her. "DeHaan Banking" in three dimensional fourteen inch high chrome plated letters were spattered with blood.

"It will be hell cleaning all of these nooks and crannies," she thought to herself staring at them. "Bad for business, definitely," her mind wandered on.

The robber in front of her turned back his skeleton mask covered with a good spraying of blood. She noticed his left eye was squinted closed. Like her, he must have gotten some material in his eye.

She raised her hands slowly.

"Please don't shoot me."

"Just don't move, we're leaving," he said calmly.

She noticed one robber pop up next to her from outside the tellers counter, his weapon high, held ready to fire.

"What happened," he said through his mask.

"Bank guard," the robber in front of her said.

"No one else gets hurt. We're leaving."

The four robbers stacked up at the door and saw their car still waiting for them. The first one eased outside and looked both ways.

"We're good," he said and the four men began to exit. After a loud popping noise from the floor, the last robber in the line crumbled to the ground, his hands not breaking his fall.

"Like a rag doll," Michelle thought.

The muscular robber turned around and fired at the man in the grey suit who was lying on the floor, missing him. The man in the grey suit fired back striking the muscular robber who was then grabbed from behind by one of the other robbers and dragged out of the bank.

As she ducked lower, she saw the man in the suit scramble to his feet and head to the door but heard two gunshots hit the thick glass and the man retreated.

"Oh my God, you're bleeding," Roger squealed at Michelle as he and the two other tellers came rushing to her.

"Call the police," Roger directed one of the other women as he took a fresh bottle of water from behind the counter.

Two other women helped her down into a desk chair.

"Put your head back."

Roger cradled her head in his shoulder. He began to slowly rinse her eye out.

Roger looked up and pointed to the man in the grey suit.

"You! You with the gun! Take his gun away," as he pointed to the dead robber on the floor. Meagan! Go lock the door honey."

Meagan, a young woman with a huge mop of curly hair and a grey chiffon dress sailed from around the counter toward the door, slipped in blood and brain. She fell into the puddle of blood. She began to cry when she noticed Larry the guard on the floor and the condition he was in. The man in the grey suit helped her to her feet and walked her to the front door.

Roger wiped the blood from Michelle's face and she could see him scanning the room.

"Is anyone else hurt," he asked.

A hush fell over the bank as the other customers started to slowly get off the floor.

Chapter 17

A Hasty Exit

Fresno, California

"Jesus Christ! What the hell happened?"

The driver sped through the neighborhood as the other three men pulled off their masks, weapons and coats and began stuffing them into their duffel bags. Dave held his stomach while Mooj tore open a gauze pad and pressed it onto the wound.

"Must have been an off duty cop or something. Carlos is dead," Dave said, his voice trailing off.

Richie was stunned.

"Fuckin' Carlos."

The driver looked at him in his rear view mirror.

"It happens," he said turning a corner quickly.

He came to a stop behind a green sport utility vehicle on a deserted street and the men quickly got out of the minivan. The driver opened the rear doors of the SUV and the men threw the bags of money and the equipment in the rear.

Richie grabbed the bucket and everyone took their cell phones, wallets and keys out. Afterwards, Richie took his and Carlos' phone.

"I'll deep six Carlos' phone once we are under way."

No one seemed to notice the remark as they were all still reeling from their mentor having just been gunned down.

"We'll split up temporarily then follow the game plan we discussed."

Once inside the green SUV, the driver slowly drove a circuitous route until he found the parking garage where all of their cars were parked. After they pulled into a parking space, the driver knelt on the seat and faced the back of the van.

"While we're lying low, everybody think about what you want to do. If you've had enough, fine. If you want to continue, we'll see how many are still on board. If anyone gets picked up, give up the playhouse. It is stocked with enough false leads to keep the cops tied up for a while. If anyone does go there with or without a warrant, we'll all get a phone call and you know the jig is up."

The driver could tell everyone heard him even though no one acknowledged what he said.

"Hey guys listen up! Today was big. There are going to be a lot of people looking for us. The F.B.I. is probably going to turn up the heat. Move slow, think before you do anything. *This* is when amateurs make mistakes. We'll get through this."

Everyone nodded and grabbed their bags except for Dave who examined his wound.

"How you doing Dave?"

"Not bad, but I'm gonna need someone to take a look at this."

"After everyone leaves I'll take you to our guy. He has treated a lot of gunshot wounds. We have him on call for things like this."

Dave nodded calmly.

"You guys get out of here. I'll be fine."

The driver put his hands up.

"Slow down, take a deep breath and let it out. We'll leave one at a time. Someone sees one man in a parking garage carrying a bag, it's nothing. Someone sees four men, well, that's something different. You first."

Mooj took Dave's hand and placed it on the gauze over his wound. "Hold it tight."

Dave nodded. Mooj stepped out. The others watched him walk to his car, start it and pull away. After a minute, Richie stepped out.

"Good luck Dave," Richie said.

"He'll be in good hands," the driver told Richie just before he slid the door closed.

As Richie merged into traffic he felt his pocket for his phone.

Without it there wasn't much chance of anyone contacting him about the meeting. If anyone did get caught, there probably wouldn't be a meeting and they were likely all on their own. There probably wasn't anything on Carlos linking him to any of the others in the gang. Maybe if the police had Mooj or Dave listed as known associates on an old arrest report somewhere they might be able to link them together. Other than that, Richie was confidant they were in the clear.

"Time to lay low," he decided as he slowly cruised away.

CHAPTER 18

TODDLER STRUCK BY AUTO

Morrow circled the parking lot looking for a parking space. He cruised slowly looking for anyone who was leaving the diner but a few people only lingered in the lot with no clear intention of getting in a car.

Over the radio a frantic dispatcher erupted over ringing phones in the background. Morrow's adrenaline surged.

"Child struck by auto 1100 Burr Road. Phones are lighting up," the dispatcher announced letting everyone know so they wouldn't be surprised by a less than immediate radio response.

"En route," Morrow said as he peeled wheels out of the parking lot.

"Two is en route," Connolly's voice boomed over the radio.

As Morrow sped to the accident the warble of his General Electric siren screamed a sense of urgency to anyone who was within ear shot. Some of the newer sirens installed in the cars over the past few years were less enthusiastic. Morrow took a deep breath before he called out of the car. Failure to do so could result in a less than manly sounding voice over the radio. Transmitting with a shaky or higher than normal pitch would leave the officer open for mocking and ridicule.

Morrow turned the corner and sped down the street toward the crowd gathered in a driveway. A woman was kneeling on the pavement holding a toddler's head off the ground screaming and rocking back and forth.

"That's got to hurt like hell kneeling on concrete like that," his mind drifted. He noticed her cell phone about a foot away from her. It was opened. As he got closer he noticed the toddler's face was devoid of color. He could see faint tire marks on the child's shirt. A mangled tricycle lay under the rear wheel of the car. Morrow grabbed his portable radio.

"Toddler run over by a car."

Grabbing the child from the woman, he tried his best to feel for a pulse. The crowd stood silently at first until one man chimed in

"Shouldn't you get him to a hospital?"

Morrow cradled the boy in his arms and pinched his nose and blew into his mouth, twice. In the distance he could hear other police cars and the ambulance coming, their sirens getting louder and louder.

"What's taking so long," another person asked while Morrow had the boy's mouth up to his ear trying to listen for a breath.

The mother jumped to her feet when she saw a green sedan speed around the corner. The driver jumped out and ran toward Morrow and the child.

"Adam! Jesus Christ NO," the man screamed.

"Adam!"

The woman grabbed the man around his waist and thrust her head to his chest

"I'm so sorry! I'm so sorry," she said as he pushed her aside and ran to the boy.

He looked at Morrow and could see in the Sergeant's eyes that the boy was dead. Morrow continued to give rescue breaths to the boy as the ambulance rolled up. Two firefighters jumped out of the ambulance and Morrow handed them the dead child. His arms dangled as did his head. The child's eyes were half open but not moving. He looked at whatever direction his head was facing.

"No lights on upstairs," Morrow thought.

The woman was on her knees begging for forgiveness; clinging to the man who was trying to get his hands on their son as he was passed off from stranger to stranger.

Connolly was suddenly standing next to Morrow while Bogard was shooing the crowd back. Amid all of the turmoil, it was as if someone cut a path through the crowd and Morrow could see a boy sitting on the front porch, calmly holding a plastic sword watching the events unfold.

Captain Fertid put his hand on Morrow's shoulder as he stared at the boy.

"You o.k.?"

Morrow nodded.

"I'm looking at this boy on the porch."

He could see Bogard talking to the boy with his hand on his back but couldn't hear what he was saying because of the ambulance pulling away with the siren on.

He could hear the chatter over the radio. The ambulance was intercepting the paramedics on the way to the hospital. Emergency room notified and waiting. The parents were gone, probably with the ambulance. The eight year old boy sat calmly.

Bogard appeared next to Morrow.

"He says he was supposed to hold his brothers hand. Mom was headed out for Chinese food for dinner."

"Crime scene tape," Morrow announced.

"Fatal accident unit needs to be notified."

Fertid took his cell phone from his ear.

"I'm on the line right now, they're en route."

Bogard tied yellow tape from the front porch next door, around the telephone pole to the mail box and ran the tape the complete width of the home where the accident occurred, tying it off on the telephone pole on the other next door neighbors yard.

"You alright?"

"Yeah. I'm starved."

Fertid and Connolly looked at Morrow who was standing with his hands on his hips. Connolly took Morrow by the arm.

"Come on. Let's get some grub."

Fertid pulled a camera out of the trunk of his unmarked car.

"You guys go eat," Fertid told Connolly. I'll hang here for the accident unit and secure the scene. I'll keep Bogard."

"Leave your car here," Connolly told Morrow

"They'll need your crime scene kit too."

Morrow got in the car with Connolly and sat back and watched the accident scene get smaller and smaller in the side view mirror.

Nestled in their corner booth at Filmore's, Morrow and Connolly scanned the menu as Sally approached.

"What were all those sirens I heard a while back? It sounded big."

Quickly burying the toddler in the back of his mind Morrow blurted out "Ambulance run for a kid. He was just feeling a little run down."

Connolly's gaze dropped onto his plate so as not to make contact with Morrow. When he did look up Morrow was looking at him with a smothered smirk.

"People call the ambulance for the damndest things these days,"

Sally remarked.

CHAPTER 19

PROUD MAMA

Santee, California

Agent Anthony Donovan sat across from the woman.

"Old school," he thought.

"Pleasant, nice house, hard working husband."

"We are so very proud of him," she said sipping tea.

"He can't really tell us much about what he does, secret stuff, dangerous I suppose, but he says there is no need to worry."

Donovan scribbled in his notebook.

"Do you have any pictures of him?"

"Oh yes. Let me get them for you," she said putting down her cup and saucer. She reminded him of his own mother.

"Tea in a cup and saucer, real plates for the cookies. None of this Styrofoam and plastic bubble boxes," he thought.

Donovan looked at the living room and spotted a portrait of her son dressed in Marine Corps dress blues, with an American flag in the background. He's seen a hundred of them; gaunt faces, blank stare of a recruit just about to graduate boot camp. He rose from the sofa and looked at the portrait. Something about it struck him. Rich looked like he was fit in the picture but "not as …" He couldn't put his finger on it.

"Here we are," she sang as she entered the room with a handful of photos. Donovan returned to the sofa and she handed him the first photo.

"This is him in his junior year of high school. He was a pretty good athlete. He pitched for the high school team and also for a travel league. He is strong and he can throw a ball like nobody's business."

"How tall is he?"

"Six foot five inches tall."

"Did he ever aspire to play professional baseball?"

"No. He made up his mind about going into the service when he was very young."

"Marines, right?"

"Yes. Right out of high school."

She handed him a few more pictures. As Donovan thumbed through them he could see the pride, athleticism and size the boy had.

"He sure is a nice looking young man," Donovan complimented the woman.

"Did you go to his graduation from boot camp?"

"No. We wanted to, but he was injured and they pushed his graduation date back because he had lost so many days. Then at the last minute they said he had enough time to graduate with his original class. It was kind of sudden. His father was very disappointed we couldn't see him graduate."

"I understand. Would it be alright if I took a picture of these photos? Just for my report."

"Sure, that's fine," she said handing him the rest of the photos. Donovan laid the photos out on the coffee table and photographed each one with his phone.

"You still haven't told me what this is about."

"We are looking for a bank robber about your son's size but obviously it isn't Richie.

"Oh, not our Rich."

"We got a call from someone who saw a news broadcast and said someone he played baseball against looked like one of the robbers in the photos; an honest mistake I am sure."

"I understand."

"Thank you for tea."

"Oh you are welcome, stop by any time."

CHAPTER 20

SMOKE AND MIRRORS

San Diego, California

"Robert Patrick in the Terminator movie," Donovan thought.

"Upright, rigid, emotionless, sharp."

"How can I help you, Sir?"

Donovan flashed his credentials at the Marine sergeant.

"Agent Donovan, F.B.I."

"Sergeant Cooper Gaudioso."

"I just wanted to verify that a Richard Armstrong joined the Marines through this recruiting station about nine months ago."

"The name rings a bell. Tall kid?"

"Six five," Donovan told him.

"Great kid. He had a problem though. What was it?"

Donovan showed him the picture on his cell phone.

"Yes. That's him. He really wanted to be a Marine; since

he was nine or ten years old."

"He didn't get in?"

"I don't believe he did," Gaudioso picked up the phone and dialed quickly.

"Staff Sergeant Blackmore, do you remember Rich Armstrong, the tall, blonde haired kid? What did he get turned down for?"

Donovan watched the sergeant while he was on the phone and began scribbling on a note pad. His uniform was spotless, crisp and tailored with a hefty stack of ribbons on his chest. He had a look about him that was hard to read.

"I believe he's doing a background check for the F.B.I. Can you hold on for a minute Staff Sergeant?"

"Can I ask what this is about?"

"We had a call that he looked like one of the bank robbers – the Skeleton Crew. They've been on the news."

"Yes. I've seen them. Do you think he is one of them," Gaudioso asked.

"I didn't until you said he was rejected. I just talked to his mother and she says he graduated boot camp and is overseas."

"She thinks he is in? I doubt it; unless he went in under a different name."

Gaudioso spoke into the phone again.

"Staff Sergeant, I'm going to have to call you back," he paused and picked up his pen and wrote a few more lines.

"I will let him know."

Hanging up the phone he looked at Donovan and seemed to be choosing his words carefully.

"He was rejected because he is lactose intolerant. Afterwards he tried to join the army, navy, air force and coast guard but they all turned him down. We have a database now and it is hard to get in if you have a physical or mental issue. It's not impossible, but we're going to look into it."

Donovan's head tilted and he took a deep breath.

"I know he took it tough, he was a bright kid. He knew more about guns and tactics and military history than some of the guys I work with. He was a hell of a gamer too."

"So as far as you know he's never been in the service."

"If he is he's using a false name."

"I have to wonder if he is one of four bank robbers and he is telling his parents he is overseas."

"It wouldn't be hard to do nowadays."

"I just hope I'm wrong."

"Sir?"

"I don't want to be the one to have to tell his mother he is not in the Marines, and robbing banks instead. She'll be crushed."

"Dangerous work. I don't envy you." Gaudioso told him.

CHAPTER 21

NIGHT COURT PLEAS

Detective Captain Fertid tapped on Chief Wilson's door and looked inside.

"Got a minute," he asked.

Wilson slid his feet off the desk and placed his fishing reel in his desk drawer and closed it.

"What's up?"

"There's been a lot of shit going on around here. The anniversary of Dick's murder is coming up, the kid who drown in the pool, the toddler who was run over, things are a little tense."

"I noticed the same thing," Wilson said wrestling with his desk chair to get comfortable.

"Things usually get tense at the height of the summer," he said taking his gun out of his holster and placing it in his desk drawer next to the fishing reel.

"What do you want to do?"

"Night court," Fertid said boldly.

"Don't even go there," Wilson said waving dismissively at the idea.

"No way."

Night court was a throwback from years before. Veteran officers remembered it. It began at seven P.M. and after their individual court cases were heard or disposed of, officers would gather at the Tiki Bar or Circus Tavern for a few, sometimes a few too many. As with many police stories, minor incidents grew over the years to major escapades where officers would commit acts of great stupidity brought on by the consumption of alcohol. Asking for a night court session was asking for trouble.

"Chief, hear me out. The guys need to relax, re-group, and get a break from everything that's been going on," Fertid said eyeing the Chief's desk drawer until Wilson took the hint and locked it with a key.

"The last time we had night court I was woken up by a goat in my kitchen." Fertid smiled.

"It's not funny," Wilson said to him.

"I know it isn't," Fertid said smiling even more broadly.

"The damn thing had his front paws on the kitchen table eating my shredded wheat and the box," Wilson reminded him.

"Not that I was in any way a party to that stunt, I have heard – rumors — that the story was a big hit with the officers. It was a real morale booster." The Chief looked at him blankly.

"Chief, do it for the guys, you know they need some leadership right now."

"No more animals. Agreed?"

"I will do everything in my power to prevent anything like that from happening again."

The Chief picked up his phone and dialed. Fertid looked at him hopefully.

"Hank," Wilson said into the phone.

"How does it look for a night court session? …for medicinal purposes."

Fertid watched as the Chief listened to whatever the Judge was saying.

"Try to get as many guys as you can, maybe pull old cases, we want to get everyone out – you know the drill."

After a moment the Chief hung up the phone.

"The court list will go up in two days."

"Excellent, that will give everyone something to look forward to," Fertid told him rising out of his chair.

"Thanks, Chief."

"No animals!"

CHAPTER 22

COURT NIGHT

The Tiki Bar was a small place adorned with tiki torches and faux thatched roofs over small, indoor huts. Plastic wicker style place mats and bamboo glasses were strewn around the bar as locals quietly drank and ate. From time to time grass skirted waitresses would come by but none of them had any hint of Pacific Islander blood.

Inside, Morrow sat at the bar sipping a beer. He was resplendent in a new, shiny blue suit with new dress shoes, shirt and tie. Bogard arrived in his black suit and went straight to the bar and pulled up a stool next to his Sergeant. Morrow looked him over up and down.

"We're pretty dressed up for a Tiki Bar."

"New suit," Bogard asked.

Morrow nodded.

"What's the occasion?"

"Why does there have to be an occasion," Morrow asked.

Big John walked in and looked at Bogard then asked loudly

"Who called for an undertaker? He's here!"

Big John took a seat on the other side of Morrow. Connolly entered. Ever since a drunken officer had flung a handful of sour cream on his suit, Bob changed before he attended after court bar get-togethers. Wearing a flannel jacket, blue jeans and work boots he threw cash on the bar.

"Where did you park your tractor, Bob," Big John asked.

"Up your ass John, there was plenty of room," Connolly replied.

Big John held up a freshly delivered beer.

"Cheers!"

Just then, a slender young woman with thick dark hair walked in and squeezed between Morrow and Bogard.

"I'll just be a minute," she said as she hailed the bartender.

"Bud," she said. Bogard and Morrow glanced at each other. The college sweatshirt was "too baggy to check out the goods" Bogard thought. However, the black stretch pants confirmed his suspicion that she was in fine shape.

"No rush," Morrow said to her. She looked up at him through heavy eyelids and smiled.

"You're a rugged looking fella, aren't you?"

He smiled at her.

"Rough night," he asked her.

"Kinda, how could you tell?"

"You look like you're on a mission?"

"Are you a cop?"

"Social worker," he lied. The young woman looked over Morrow's shoulder and could see herself and Bogard in the mirror.

"Tell your friend behind me my pants are about to burst into flames from his heat vision."

Bogard pretended he didn't hear the remark but moved away from the young woman.

Morrow's world suddenly shrunk to encompass two bar stools and the tiny piece of real estate they shared. A few drinks, a pair of shots, at the young ladies request, and Morrow experienced the best kind of tunnel vision a drunken single man can experience. The last he was seen, Morrow was leaning over talking into her ear and she was laughing at whatever he said. Bogard, Connolly and Big John moved a few feet away as soon as they could what was happening. From time to time Bogard would look up and see Morrow laughing with his new friend. As the music played, and time went on, Morrow and the young woman disappeared un-noticed.

Morrow was not missed although the woman and her stretch pants were. The officers made the best of it by drinking shots, telling stories and jokes and unwinding.

"So Dick is unconscious, his head and arm hanging out the rear passenger window of my car. He had vomited on the windshield. Once I got him in the car I turned on the windshield wipers and guess what."

Bogard shook his head. Connolly smiled having heard the story a dozen times before.

"I turn on the windshield wipers and they smear the vomit all over the windshield but there is no windshield wiper fluid. So I'm driving down the White Horse Pike, this head and arm hanging out the car, vomit smeared ALL over the windshield and I stop at a red light. The three girls pull up next to me and the driver looks at Dick, the vomit and then at me. I give her my best *hey baby* look and she and the other girls laugh and then go through the red light."

About ten other officers were just a few feet away huddled in a group. Bogard could hear them chanting "one-two-three," and there seemed to be some sort of quick motion with one officer's hands and someone would yell "fuuuuuuck!" He tried to see what was going on but couldn't from his bar stool. Big John nodded toward the bartender and when Bogard looked, he could see him filling nine shot glasses with water and the other one with tequila. Bogard and Connolly laughed as Big John shook his head and a young man in a college sweatshirt and sweatpants pushed his way between them.

"Excuse you," Bogard said sarcastically. The young man looked at him with disdain and then flagged the bartender.

"What do you need," the bartender asked him abruptly.

"I'm looking for a girl," he answered.

"Every man in here is looking for a girl. What makes you so special," Bogard cracked.

Frustrated, the college aged man shoved Bogard to the

ground.

"Whoaa, ass hole!" Connolly said as he grabbed the man by his arm.

The college man was actually Pete Conway, star wrestler from the local college, and not accustomed to being manhandled. Conway swung his arm out of Connolly's grasp and shoved him back. Bogard grabbed Conway from behind and tried to place him in a choke hold which Conway countered by bending forward and flipping Bogard over his shoulder. By now several of the Greenlee officers were advancing on the man. Big John was able to grab Conway's hand and squeeze it forcing him to the ground. Conway countered by falling to the floor and spinning out of the arm lock Big John was placing him in. He then punched Big John in the groin bringing him to his knees. From behind, one officer slapped a large handful sour cream in his face.

"Have some sour cream, jerk off," one officer yelled.

"Here is some beer to wash it down with," another yelled as he poured beer over Conway's head.

Conway continued to try to pull his hand from Big John's grip to no avail. He struggled mightily and suddenly was released from the grip. Conway flew backwards into the fluorescent lights in the juke box, breaking them. He stood up, holding his hand under his armpit, face aglow with beer and sour cream. He raised his middle finger.

"Fuck you all!"

From the rear of his truck in the parking lot, Morrow saw a young man being chased by a crowd of well dressed off duty police officers. When the man got a clear picture of his situation, he hastily climbed in his car.

Morrow, still lying on top of the young woman, saw approximately a dozen off duty police officers pounding on a small car with a the man inside. Suddenly they began rocking the car back and forth. Other officers were shooing patrons back into the bar.

"I'll be right back," Morrow said dismounting from the woman and exiting his truck.

As he approached the officers

"Yo guys," he yelled as the car flipped over on its roof.

"You guys, you can't –,"

As the crowd spun the car around in a circle, with the man still trapped inside, sirens were heard, close by and getting closer by the second. The intoxicated mob fled to the beach. Morrow could see headlights turning into the parking lot and decided after careful consideration to flee with the rest of the officers.

The group fled in three different directions, north on the beach, south on the beach and a small group ran into the ocean. Gary Geeman and Doug O'Malley lay in the ocean watching as the police cars arrived in the parking lot several hundred feet away. Big John jumped into the water and lazily floated on his back.

Of the group that ran south, most dispersed into the dune area and hid in dune grass and mulberry bushes watching from the distance. Spotlights could be seen taking large swipes through the dark neighborhood.

Morrow, Connolly and Bogard ran south on the beach stopped for a moment to watch two patrol cars drive by. As the three men tried to work their way back toward the road, they were forced into the marshes. Morrow cringed as he felt the water riding knee high on his pants. The mud and muck seeped into his brand new black leather shoes. Morrow took his cell phone out of his pocket and held it just over the water line as he, Connolly, and Bogard squatted down in the water and bay reeds as one patrol car stopped and swept the area with its spot light. Connolly, fully submersed in the water looked over at Morrow and Bogard.

"I'll bet you didn't think we'd go swimming tonight."

In the darkness, the three men sat, lit only by a random pass of the searching officers. Connolly knew Morrow was squeamish when it came to sea creatures.

"I sure hope there aren't any creatures in this water," Connolly said to the other two.

"Stop that talk right now," Morrow warned.

"It's not funny. If I didn't have shoes on I'd either be giving myself up or dead of fright," Morrow whispered.

Bogard settled into the muck.

"I'm thinking this suit might be ruined."

"I'm thinking you're right," Connolly told him.

Morrow slid over behind the other two men. He dialed his phone.

"Who the hell are you calling?"

Connolly could see Morrows smile in the glow of the cell phone.

Sally sat up in bed panicked when she heard the phone ring and looked at the time "1:15 A.M."

As her panic subsided her curiosity kicked in. She answered.

"Hello?"

She looked at the clock and then at her dress hanging on the closet door. She could hear Morrow's voice but he was whispering.

"Did I wake you?"

"Kind of," she said trying not to sound harsh.

"I'm sorry, we're in a little bit of a jam."

"What's wrong?"

"We're in the marshes off of Bay Shore Avenue."

Sally could hear the water. It sounded like someone wading through thigh deep water, maybe even trying to run. A rustling or bristling was also audible over the phone.

"Any particular reason?"

"Running from the cops."

"You are the cops," Sally reminded him.

"Well, not tonight. Would it be possible for you to pick us up?"

"Sure. Where?"

"How about the parking lot by the Pirates Inn restaurant?"

"Give me about ten minutes."

Morrow closed his phone and told Bogard and Connolly

"We have ten minutes to make it to the Pirates Inn. Sally will pick us up there."

Connolly grinned.

"She's a real peach isn't she?"

Bogard looked at the roadway.

"Someone is out of their car, coming this way."

The three men sank down to their necks completely submersing their suits in the bay water. A hand held flashlight swept their way.

"I think he heard you on the phone," Bogard told Morrow.

They watched as a uniformed officer climbed over the bulkhead and onto some large boulders which sat half exposed in the water. To their horror, they watched as the officer slipped, fell onto the rock and slipped into the dark water, his flashlight dropping into the darkness.

After the rush of water they could hear him.

"Mother fucker!!!"

Another officer stepped over the bulkhead, held onto it then shined his light on the wet officer.

"Give me your hand" he yelled and pulled the drenched cop from the marshes.

"Fuck ME!" he yelled once he got to dry land.

"These guys are pissed," Connolly whispered.

"Who was it?"

"Can't tell."

Sally drove down Bay Shore Avenue wearing her bathrobe and the glasses that no one ever saw. They were for down time. Late night cross word puzzles or Sudoku, this would come as a shock when the boys saw her. Red and blue lights swirled and flashed behind her. A spotlight reflected off of her rear view mirror.

"Cops," she thought.

"This isn't good."

Patrolman Theo Papadopoulos got out of the car holding his flashlight and stood next to the police car. Sally could see him calling her license plate in to the dispatcher.

"Documented," she thought.

After a moment Theo walked up to her car and shined the light in her eyes.

"Sally. "

"Good morning Officer," she said smiling.

"Why on God's green earth are you out and about at this time of night?"

"I'm old enough to be out after curfew," she teased.

"Is everything o.k.? Was I speeding?"

"No. We're looking for some kids who beat up someone and flipped his car over."

"Hooligans," she asked.

"Sounds like it to me," he answered smiling.

"How long have you worn glasses? They're nice."

"About thirty years. I don't usually wear them out of the house. I wear contact lenses."

"You must have been in some kind of hurry," he said trying to press her for an answer.

She exhaled deeply.

"Tampons. I'm going to get tampons."

Theo cringed and spun to his right.

"I'm sorry to have held you up," he said as he walked back to his car.

Sally watched him turn off his lights and make a u-turn. She pulled away and headed to the all night convenience store and pulled into the lot. She waited for less than a minute and saw Theo drive by in his patrol car.

"Checking up on me," she thought.

Inside the store a young clerk looked at Sally and her bathrobe.

Sally stormed down the aisle and scooped up a box of tampons. She put them on the counter and pulled a ten dollar bill out of her pocket and handed it to the clerk.

"Sally?"

"Yes? Oh, I didn't recognize you," she said. It was one of her semi regulars, ham and cheese omelet and decaf with rye toast.

"New glasses?"

"No. I don't usually wear them in public."

"I see," the clerk stated indicating she knew why.

Sally grabbed the tampons and left abruptly.

A young man walked from the small office behind the counter.

"That was rude."

"She's on her period, cut her a break."

Sally wheeled her car around the lot onto Bay Shore Avenue and found her way to the Pirates Inn. She pulled into the lot, backed in and shut off her lights. As she waited, she thought about their friendship and what it meant to her. Certainly what they pulled off at the Vincelli trial was extraordinary and looking back, quite foolish. She knew that what they did, they did together out of respect for Dick Cambridge and his family, but also through a sense of justice. Vincelli had done everything the easy way; dealing drugs, extorting protection money, and when he got caught, murdered witnesses, and Dick Cambridge. She wondered how they had gotten away with it. Some seemed suspicious of Connolly, Morrow and Big John. They either condoned what they did or, perhaps thinking they were capable of murder, decided not to press the issue. Either way, it seemed to be over; except for the lingering worry that someday, someone would feel the need to clear their conscience, come forward, spill the beans and send all of them to prison.

Tap tap tap. Sally looked up at Morrow who was wearing a beautiful blue suit, soaking wet, covered in sand and mud. Connolly and Bogard stood behind him both having been submerged and rolled in sand.

"Somebody call for a cab," she asked.

"Yes. Do you mind," he said motioning to his wet, sandy suit.

"Hop in. A good friend of mine is paying to have my car detailed tomorrow."

Morrow jumped in the front seat, Connolly and Bogard jumped in the back. Sally began driving slowly.

Taking a circuitous route she dodged all of the police cars still out on the prowl. Suddenly, back lit by a far off street light, a figure emerged stumbling from the dunes.

"Big foot? A bear? A sloth," she wondered. As she slowed Big John staggered up and put his palms on the hood of her car.

"Police emergency, I'm commandeering this car," he said.

"Like hell you are. Put your fat ass in the back," she told him.

"Sally? What are you doing out?"

She turned the interior light on to show him she had Morrow, Connolly and Bogard with her.

"Johnny-on-the-spot," he said then climbed in the rear hatch of her car.

"What the hell happened," she asked as she started moving again.

"Some dipshit came in and started some trouble with Bogard," Big John said.

"I got a hold of him but he kicked me in the stones."

Sally's face melted into a grimace.

"All I saw was some poor bastard in his upside down car being spun around on his roof," Morrow admitted.

"The bar was busted up pretty good," Bogard chimed in. He was glad to be a part of the shenanigans. There was closeness within the group he couldn't quite put his finger on; Morrow, Big John, Bob Connolly, Sally and even Jack Duffield when he was around. It was as if they were all in on some sort of joke or something. This time he was in the thick of it. He liked it.

Morrow looked over at Sally.

"How long have you been wearing glasses?"

"I wear them at home after I take my contact lenses out. You never saw me in these. Do you understand?"

"I do. I'm sorry I mentioned it. I know it isn't a good time for you," he added.

"What's that supposed mean?"

Morrow picked up the box of tampons from the floor of the car, showed them to her and put them down discretely.

"No. I got pulled over on the way here and that was the excuse I made for being out at this hour. It worked but Theo rode by the store to see if I was stopping or not, so I bought them. "

Sally pulled up in front of Connolly's home.

"Say hi to your wife for me."

"Will do. Thanks Sally," Connolly said climbing out of the back seat his wet shoes making a sucking noise as he stepped out.

Sally pulled away from the curb and headed to Big John's house. Within minutes he was asleep in the back of the station wagon. His snoring sounded like a farm animal. Gas rolled out from the other end. Bogard requested, and received, an airing out of the passenger compartment of the car.

"Four fourty air conditioning. That's what we used to call it. Four windows down forty miles an hour," Morrow said aloud. Sally noticed how talkative he was.

"It probably has something to do with the overpowering smell of liquor in the car," she thought.

Big John's wife was on the front porch when Sally pulled in front of his house.

"What happened to him," she asked as she looked in the rear window.

"I don't know. We found him like this," Morrow lied. Cindy looked at him and seeing he was soaking wet and covered with sand as her husband was, decided not to push the issue.

Bogard and Morrow took an arm and started walking him to the front door. Big John pulled away from them.

"Come on tough guy," his wife said pushing him in the right direction.

Morrow stuck his head out of the window as the car was pulling away from the curb.

"The cops are looking for us so keep him quiet until he sobers up."

After a short trip a few blocks over, Sally dropped off Bogard at his home and pulled away. At the corner she turned right instead of left, the direction of Morrow's house. She looked straight ahead while she was driving. Morrow wondered if it was a lapse in concentration. Maybe it was because she was woken up in the middle of the night. He didn't know. All he did know was, he was wet, covered in sand of which several grains had found their way into his underwear. He was sure his shoes were shrinking and that he had a young woman in the back of his truck at the bar. She was probably asleep by now if she hadn't left. He was intrigued.

Sally made her way toward her own house, pulled into her driveway, and shut off the engine.

"I need you to do something for me."

CHAPTER 23

THE MORNING AFTER

Sally rounded the corner and pulled into the Tiki Bar parking lot. Morrow noticed his back windows were still rolled down from the night before. He looked at Sally and she looked at him and took a deep breath and opened her mouth. As she was about to say something movement from inside the truck caught his eye. Not only his eye but Sally's as well. The young college girl, the subject of the words between Bogard and Conlin, the pushing shoving, punching and ultimately the flipping of his vehicle and the subsequent manhunt by the duty officers, was still in the backseat of his truck.

"Awkward," he thought.

"Get out," Sally said looking at him with contempt.

"I knew you'd come back," the young woman said upon seeing Morrow getting dropped off. She scrunched her face and made two fists and thrust them outward as she yawned.

"I knew you'd come back," she said smiling, unaware of Sally's disapproval.

Morrow climbed out of the car and leaned in the window and struggled for the right words. It wasn't necessary.

"I have to get to work," Sally said looking straight ahead and putting her car in gear.

"O.K. see you soon," he said uneasily.

CHAPTER 24

MISSING CHILD

Captain Fertid sat across from the Chief. Looking at him he could tell he was not happy. The fight, with the local college wrestling star made headlines in the local paper and TV news. The over-turned car in the parking lot was reminiscent of those wild riots often associated with European Soccer bouts. The Chief suspected a few off duty officers were involved. At least there weren't any animals involved.

As he read the account of the brawl on his computer screen, he didn't acknowledge Captain Fertid. The Captain braced for the worst.

"Hundreds of dollars worth of damage," the Chief stated still looking at his monitor. Fertid folded his arms.

"Overturned vehicle…Swollen eye, fat lip, possible elbow sprain; several suspects escaped on foot," Wilson read aloud then looked at Fertid.

"Yes sir," Captain Fertid responded, "We're still looking into it."

As the Chief looked at him, he said nothing but his eyes asked

"Are you shitting me?" Fertid shot back with his best "whatever are you talking about" look.

After a brief moment Wilson spoke.

"Are you going to pretend that you have no suspicions that our officers were involved?"

"Yes, for as long as I can I am," Fertid told him.

The Chief finally cracked a smile.

"Chief, go walk around downstairs for a few minutes. There is a buzz today. It's something we haven't seen around here in a while. It reminds me of when Dick Cambridge was here, with some of the shit he used to pull."

The Chief got up and looked out the window.

"I know. Something to distract them from all of the crap that's happened here lately. Come here, quick," Wilson said.

Fertid moved to the window and could see four officers in the parking lot, one of them rocking an imaginary car and flipping it over. The other three officers laughed.

"Get Morrow in here. I'm going to make him sweat a little," the Chief said smiling.

Fertid picked up the phone,

"Have Sergeant Morrow signal the Chiefs office," dropping the phone on the receiver he asked

"What are you going to do?"

"I am going to put him in charge of following up on the incident. The guys on the twelve to eight shift can't follow up because of their hours."

"You *are* a ball buster."

"I have my moments," the Chief admitted.

Morrow walked in with a cup of coffee in his hand. Good morning," he said mustering his most innocent smile.

"Have a seat Sergeant," Wilson told him. Taken aback by his formality, Morrow sat down and held his coffee cup in front of him with two hands. Fertid sat next to him looking at the Chief who was now looking at his computer monitor.

Morrow sat quietly, worried.

"They must know," he thought.

"They HAVE to know. Maybe the bartender told the night shift guys what happened. Maybe one of the Chief's relatives was in the bar. Maybe…"

"Sergeant," the Chief said abruptly.

"Thursday night, there as an incident at the…"

he stopped and continued reading the report on his computer. Fertid looked at Morrow briefly and then turned away smiling.

"The incident where," Morrow wondered.

"Fuck! Fuck! Fuck," he thought letting his breath out slowly through his nose.

"At the bar, the brawl" the Chief stopped still focused on

the screen. Morrow's heart raced.

"District one and district three, prepare to copy," the dispatcher's voice came over the radio.

"Go ahead," Bogard replied.

"Eight one one Sterling Place, missing child, five years old blonde female wearing denim overalls and a pink t-shirt."

"En route, I'm about two blocks away," Bogard said over the radio. Chief Wilson, Captain Fertid and Sergeant Morrow all began leaving the Chief's office.

"Tell him to check the house thoroughly as soon as he gets there. We'll check the area with the other district cars" Wilson told Morrow. Morrow relayed the order over the radio.

"Will do," Bogard replied.

"I'll try to get the fire department and public works to get any available people in the area too," the Chief told Morrow. Fertid pulled his keys from his pocket.

"I'll check the area then go to the house."

Officer Bogard pulled up to the home and a nice looking woman of about forty met him at the curb. "Officer I can't find my daughter."

"Alright ma'am, when was the last time you saw her?"

"About forty five minutes ago."

"Are there any custody issues we should know about?"

"My husband and I are separated but he would never do

anything like this."

"O.K. Let's check the house, the other units are on the way and they will be looking for her."

As Bogard and the child's mother began searching the house they could hear the radio transmissions over Bogard's portable radio.

"All units, public works has two pickup trucks in the area, where would you like them to concentrate?"

"Along the golf course."

"I'll pass it on to them."

"Fire department has two men in the area in the Chiefs car."

"Ask them to check the side streets in the immediate area."

"I'll be checking with the father to see if he knows anything," Connolly reported.

"Bob, he's living with his father on Travis Place," Morrow told him.

"Affirm, I'm there now, he's pretty upset. I'll be bringing him to Sterling place to help with the search."

Sergeant Morrow drove by a public works truck parked on the side of the road. He looked on the golf course and saw one of the workers wading in the pond. He then waved the sergeant on.

O'Malley sat at the foot of the bridge eyeballing cars driving by. Sometimes by leering at traffic he could evoke a reaction from drivers. So far no one seemed unusual.

All of the officers on duty knew the missing girl. Her mom was a dealer at one of Atlantic City's casinos; her father was an auto mechanic. They seemed to be a nice stable family but the month before, the father moved out.

"Number eleven to Officer Bogard, did you check the house yet?"

"We're doing it now, so far U.T.L."

Morrow drove out to the bridge and saw O'Malley sitting there.

"Good," he thought. It was nice when someone took it upon themselves to monitor traffic leaving Greenlee.

O'Malley sat in his car trying to imagine what a man would look like if he passed a police car with a dead or unconscious child duct taped in the back. Would they look at him? Would they instinctively turn away? Would they try to flee? Would he give chase with a small child in the car? He sat and stared at the cars leaving the island sizing up each driver. He knew most of them.

Detective Fritz unlocked the filing cabinet and pulled out eight files and placed them on his desk. Registered sex offenders; a few eighteen year old men with 15 year old girlfriends, a chronic masturbator and one man who, fifteen years ago had propositioned a thirteen year old girl who was actually a thirty five year old prosecutors office investigator. It was a place to start. He texted the Chief.

"Sorting through the registered sex offenders. Nothing really fits but starting with Lance on Montpelier Avenue."

"K," was the only reply from the Chief.

Two other district cars rolled through the area, checking playgrounds, schoolyards and backyard pools in the area. Checking with children, letter carriers and power walkers and runners, no one had seen the girl.

Chief Wilson entered the front door and saw Bogard taking notes from the mother.

"Bev," he said to her, "is there anyone who may have come by, or a friends' house she may have gone to?"

Beverly shook her head back and forth. Captain Fertid walked in.

"Hey Beverly, we have a lot of people looking for your daughter. Stacey?"

"Yes. Stacey Marie."

"You checked the house,? the Chief asked Bogard.

"Yes. I checked the house, the crawl space, the attic, and the shed."

O'Malley noticed a white Mercury headed toward him, speeding just a little. Not something he would normally pay attention to. He waited for the car to get closer to gauge the drivers reaction. He looked at him. A hard look. A challenge. Almost a threat. The driver looked back at him and then straight ahead as if spooked. O'Malley put his car in gear and rapidly pulled into traffic. As he weaved through a few other vehicles he found his spot behind the white Mercury, turned on his overhead lights and the driver pulled over to the side of the road.

O'Malley approached the driver and asked for his

paperwork. He noticed the man was tubby, soft looking with a comb over. Suspicious, O'Malley wondered, "Who wears a comb over these days? With so many bald notable athletes, celebrities and public figures, who tries to hide their baldness anymore?"

The man handed him his paperwork neatly paper clipped together. "Tidy; Maybe too tidy," the Patrolman noticed.

"Was I speeding officer," the driver asked.

"Yes sir," was the only reply. O'Malley looked him over. "Nervous," he thought.

"Would you step out of the vehicle please?" The driver quickly got out of the car and was escorted to the side of the road. O'Malley glanced at the trunk. The driver's eyes followed O'Malley's.

"Something wrong," the man asked. His pasty white skin and comb over cemented what appeared to be a very nerdy person who wore his pants hiked up to his belly button and a v-neck velour shirt which did nothing to hide the driver's man boobs.

"Do you know why I stopped you?"

"Speeding?"

O'Malley waited a few seconds to increase the stress. He spoke slowly and deliberately.

"Do you know why I *really* stopped you?"

The man smiled.

"I am really flattered. Really I am, but I don't go that way." O'Malley's eyes widened.

"No! Oh God no," the officer blurted out.

"I'm straight. I'm not really the most macho guy in the world but—"

"Wait a minute. That's not where I was going. There's a missing girl, five years old, everyone is looking for her."

"Oh Jesus that's awful! You think that I? Me?" the man stammered.

"Can I look in your trunk? You don't have to let me," O'Malley told him.

"No. Go ahead. By all means. Get back out there and find that girl."

O'Malley had the man step away from him while he retrieved the keys and popped the trunk lid. The man looked at him. O'Malley pulled the lid open. He looked inside and was met by a horrific odor. It was a powerful, rotting stench. He stepped back, aghast.

Back at the house Bob Connolly walked in with Stacey's father who immediately hugged his estranged wife. Captain Fertid, Chief Wilson and Officer Bogard gauged his reaction. It seemed genuine enough. His eyes welled up but his wife broke down sobbing.

"I don't know what to do," she cried. As he hugged his wife, his eye caught something slight. A kitchen cabinet seemed to move slightly, then about an inch, then a few more inches. He saw blonde hair, a blue eye and then a small hand popped out and gave him a gentle wave.

"Hi dad," she whispered with a broad smile.

"Stacey Marie!" he yelled startling everyone. He let go of

his wife and opened the cabinet and pulled the tiny girl out and hugged her. She squeezed him tightly. Beverly squealed and grabbed her and squeezed her and began crying even harder.

Chief Wilson looked at Bogard. The young officer was dumbfounded. Captain Fertid shook his head in disdain. The Chief put his radio to his mouth while still looking at Bogard.

"All cars, the missing child has been located. All is well." As the numerous police, fire, public works employees answered, Detective Fritz stepped off stepped off a porch. As he walked away from the house, a man opened the door.

"Can I help you?"

"No. Sorry. Wrong address."

Officer O'Malley waited for the driver to buckle his seatbelt before returning his paperwork.

"Well I'm glad she's ok. That is very upsetting to think of someone abducting a little girl."

"Yes it is," O'Malley said breathing a little easier.

"I'm sorry about the clams in my trunk. I forgot they were there. They've been there about week."

"Not a problem."

"And imagine, I thought you were hitting on me."

O'Malley shook his head.

"That'll be our little secret," O'Malley warned him.

"Oh you bet," the man said with a wink.

25

Skeleton Crew On the Run

Longway, Arizona

Mooj drove the minivan down the barren desert highway while Dave lay across the back seat. Still sore from his gut shot and patch job, he winced whenever there was a sudden turn, stop, or bump in the road. Richie was in the way back of the minivan.

The driver took a rare break from driving and sat up front in the passenger seat.

"What are you looking for," he asked Richie.

"Just checking out what we're riding with."

Richie pulled out a large professional looking video camera from its protective crate.

"Sweet," he said.

"We have a movie camera, lights, clap board and reflective umbrella."

Mooj looked at him through the rear view mirror.

"Whatcha gonna do with it?"

"Maybe while Dave is immobilized we should take advantage of him and make a snuff film," Richie said.

"If you touch me in any other way than a manly handshake, I'll stick that camera so far up your ass you'll be able to video tape your hopes and dreams."

Richie smiled and continued examining the camera. Dave

lay back on the seat.

"Richie," he said still trying to find a comfortable position.

"What are you in this for? You seem like you got a lot going for you, unlike us."

"You guys are great. We have a lot of fun, we're making lots of money…"

"Traveling to exotic places," Mooj added.

"Yes, that too," Richie agreed.

"I mean, what are you in it for? I like the casinos, Mooj here; he's trying to pay his way back to Pakistan."

"Fuck you, Dave," Mooj yelled from the front.

"I ain't no Pakistani."

"Well whatever the fuck you are- I just can't figure you out."

Richie began trying to put the camera back in the box the way he found it.

"I have a friend, a bit older than me; he's all fucked up from the war in Iraq. He was like a big brother to me; a great baseball player too. He showed me how to throw a curve ball when I was about eight years old. I mean really showed me and practiced with me. I had a lot of success with it. I was a few years ahead of anyone in my league at the time."

Dave popped his head up "So that made you want to rob banks?"

"Well, he joined the army, went to Iraq, got blown up and

lost his legs and a few fingers, fractured his skull. His mind is just shattered and the Veterans Administration keeps putting him off, losing his paperwork, and just basically trying to give him the brush off. He'll never be the same but I figure I can get him some help, modern prosthetics, even get him laid once in a while."

"Must have been a good friend," Mooj said, resting his head while still driving.

"He was," Richie said.

"*Is*," he caught himself.

"Funny how I think of him in the past tense sometimes. He's not the same, not even close but I just feel like the old Clay is in there somewhere and he knows I know that."

A hush fell over the van and the four men drifted into their own thoughts. Richie climbed forward into the back seat with Dave and watched out the window as a steady flow of neon signs whizzed by.

"You know the sad thing," Richie said.

"Other than losing your legs and fucking up your mind and being given the brush off? No. What is the sad thing?"

"My grandfather went through something similar. He had been in the army. He had cancer and it was due to Agent Orange. He was around it all the time but they wouldn't acknowledge it. He fought, wrote letters to congress, hired lawyers, joined law suits, the whole bit, but to him it wasn't real unless they admitted it."

The driver piped in.

"Why the fuck would you wait for someone else to validate what you know?"

"For him to admit he was being screwed on purpose he would have to come to the realization that everything he had been taught about our country, our values, our way of life was fantasy. That's a tough leap to make."

"Let me tell you something," Mooj said,

"This is the greatest country in the world. Believe me."

"I know it is," Richie told him "but we have problems."

"Tell him how tough you had it in Pakistan, Mooj," Dave chimed in.

"I'm not from Pakistan you stupid prick," Mooj yelled.

"I'm from Indonesia!"

'So Mooj is an Indonesian name," Richie asked.

"Mooj is a nickname Dave gave me. I don't know what it means."

"It's short for Mujahedeen."

Mooj looked at Dave in the rear view mirror.

"Dave. I am going to kill you slowly. First I am going to drive over every pot hole I see. Every one!"

CHAPTER 26

STATE TROOPER VS. THE SKELETON CREW

Longway, Arizona

Trooper James Bustamante took the first bite of his sandwich and took a big gulp of his purple juice. He looked over his dashboard at the radar unit. Nothing. He continued to eat. Air conditioning on high, radio tuned to his favorite talk show he tilted the driver's seat back one click. His body armor constricted his breathing. It was hot and his t-shirt was damp and stuck to his skin. He grabbed the top of the vest of it and pulled it out and back, out and back trying to force the hot air out and allow some of the cooler air in.

In the distance he could see a vehicle headed his way. The highway was level and straight and the desert on both sides was barren. The rock formations far out in the distance were post card beautiful.

Bustamante eyed the vehicle and watched as the radar flashed the reading. Ninety, eighty nine, ninety, eighty nine. As it approached he took a bite of his sandwich. No hurry.

There was really nowhere to go. The worst that could happen is the driver and one of the passengers could switch places. Maybe throw a bag of dope out the window. Taking a swig of his purple juice, he packed his cooler.

"Fuuuuuuuck," Mooj said as he blew by the highway patrol car parked on the side of the road.

"We're gonna get stopped," he said panicking.

"Our ID's will hold up, everyone stay calm," the driver said.

Half sitting, half laying across the backseat, Dave reached down and felt the handgun under his leg. Richie looked at him and then out of the back window.

"Nothing yet," he announced.

Mooj began to back it down slowly.

"Let's see if he comes after us."

Dave checked again and felt relieved.

"All clear," he told everyone else.

Bustamante stowed his cooler on the floor. He leaned forward and brought the back of his seat up one click. He tugged on his seatbelt to double check it was locked in. Scanning the area he put his car in gear and let the idle pull him onto the road.

"Ready hon," he asked the car. The low grumbling of the engine indicated she was.

He stepped on the gas pedal and propelled the car forward at such a speed that he caught up to the minivan in several seconds.

"Ho-lee shit! Where'd he come from," Mooj asked once he noticed the highway patrol car behind him and keeping up with him. Dave checked his shirt to make sure blood wasn't seeping through.

Mooj pulled the van over to the side of the road. Bustamante called in the license plate number and got out of his car and approached the minivan. Mooj handed the trooper his paperwork before he could ask for it.

"I'm really sorry officer. I know I was speeding."

"Yes you were," Bustamante replied eyeing Mooj and then the others.

"I don't usually drive on such wide open roads like this. It doesn't seem like you're going that fast because there really isn't any landmarks to gauge your speed."

"I know what you mean."

Dave watched the officer from the back seat. In his mind he rehearsed the motion of grabbing his gun and shooting the officer if things got out of hand. Richie admired the officer's uniform. Neat, tailored, pressed. Despite the vest he still looked trim. Obviously he worked out; leather gear looked fairly new but broken in. A forty five sat in the holster. Another smaller gun might be sitting in his left front pants pocket. Mirrored sunglasses gave the Trooper a slight advantage as no one knew exactly where he was looking.

Bustamante looked squarely at Dave.

"Can I see some identification?"

"Me," Dave asked.

"You. Is there a problem?"

"No. I was just curious as to why."

"No seatbelt," Bustamante said holding his hand slightly inside the van indicating he wanted the papers pronto. Dave looked down and noticed the officer was right.

"This is how it starts," Dave thought remembering all of the stories he had heard about road cops finding the smallest little thing to investigate and then turning up big prizes. Money, guns, dope, you name it. Stopping a car for a bad inspection sticker and the next thing you know they are dismantling the car and removed the hundreds of pounds of cocaine from inside.

Dave gingerly rolled to his right and took his wallet out of his left back pocket cautiously so as not to expose the gun under his right leg. The pain from the gunshot wound, the stitches, and moving after hours of sitting motionless in the back of the van caused Dave to wince.

"Something wrong?"

"No sir. Just a little banged up from softball."

The officer looked at him through his mirrored glasses. Dave wondered what he was thinking.

"How'd you do that?"

"Collision at home plate. I tried to bowl the catcher over trying to score. Bad idea on my part."

Dave handed him his identification. The officer took it

and noticed Richie looking at his hand.

Richie could see the reflection of himself in the mirrored glasses. He could also see Dave looking uncomfortably at the cop.

Mooj looked into the side view mirror and could see the cop's gun.

"Safety holster," he thought.

The driver waited to hear the gunshot. Whether it was Dave or the cop, he was expecting it.

"I'll be back in a minute."

The officer stepped backward and walked back to his car.

"There's no way this van has been entered as stolen yet. I picked it up from the long term parking at the airport," the driver said.

"We'll find out in a minute," Mooj said. He could hear Dave taking the safety off of his Smith and Wesson nine millimeter.

"Easy," the driver told him.

Suddenly the officer got out of the car and began walking up.

"If it came back a hit he'd just cover down on us."

Bustamante handed Mooj his paperwork and Dave's.

"Slow down. Everybody put your seatbelts on."

"Thanks officer," Mooj said putting his paperwork back in his wallet. As the officer walked away Mooj stuck his head out the window.

"How far to the next gas station?"

"About five miles from here. Indian Joe's filling station. You low?"

"We'll make five miles with no problem. Thanks officer."

Mooj pulled away slowly despite the adrenalin running through his veins.

Bustamante sat in his car and watched the minivan pull away. He opened his purple juice and took a sip. On his patrol log he noted the time, location and reason for the traffic stop. He grabbed his microphone and was about to transmit when the dispatcher called him.

"Jim, what's your status?"

"Clearing now. Whattaya got?"

"That minivan. You still got it in sight?"

"Not really but it can't be more than a couple miles down the road. Why?"

"Stolen. Just came in. Possible bad ass robbery crew using it."

"Are these the guys travelling with the wounded guy?"

"That's them".

Bustamante realized the softball player in the back seat was most likely nursing a bullet wound. Bustamante let out a sigh.

"Son-of-a-BITCH!"

He pressed the transmit button on the microphone.

"Let everyone know they're headed east. They might be stopped off at Indian Joe's for gas. I'll head up there."

"Be careful James," the Dispatcher warned.

"Will do."

Indian Joe slept in the old wooden chair in front of his road side gas station. Looking more like a road side ghost town than an actual gas station, Indian Joe's was a stopping point where motorists gassed up before going over a hundred miles before the next filling station. Here was gas, take it or leave it. There wasn't any reason to gouge people. Indian Joe didn't have high overhead. No fancy new signs, computerized pumps, or cappuccino machines. He had gas, a few snacks and cold drinks. Indian Joe liked it that way.

He'd given away more gas jugs to strangers than he could remember but it was a small price to pay for such a cushy job. Sitting watching the clouds roll through slowly and the never changing landscape across the road. His solitude was broken only by motorists from time to time and an occasional paperback novel.

Bustamante pulled into the lot and saw Indian Joe sitting, maybe sleeping in the chair out front.

"Hey Joe, did you have a minivan come through here the past few minutes?"

"Nope, why?"

"Four malo hombres wanted for bank robbery and murder are in a minivan are in the area. I just stopped them a few minutes ago."

"Why didn't you arrest them," Indian Joe asked, needling the officer.

"Had I known it at the time, I would have."

"Oh, I see," Joe said in a very slightly condescending tone with a hint of a smirk.

"Don't start your shit with me Joe. These are bad dudes."

Indian Joe could see Bustamante wasn't his usual self.

"I'll keep an eye out for them. What do they look like?"

"One's brown, like an Indian."

"Native American or the ones the Pakistanis like to hate?"

"The latter. Another one is a young kid, tall, real tall. One muscle head. He might be shot in the stomach and a regular looking Joe."

"If I see them I will call the station if you want."

"Fine. They were in a green minivan with California tags."

"O.K. Hope you get them."

"Me too," Bustamante said pulling away.

Indian Joe had never seen him so serious. Joe wondered if he shouldn't have teased him.

"Nah," he thought after a half a second of consideration.

Joe sat back in his chair and picked up his paperback and put his feet on a wooden crate. As he thumbed through the pages looking for the spot where he left off, he saw a familiar green extended cab pickup truck veer off the road into the lot. He dropped his book and slowly tore himself out of the chair. As he approached the driver it wasn't who he expected.

"Can I help you?"

"Filler up with regular," the young man said. The brown man next to him was looking at a map.

"Sure thing," Joe said moving to the rear of the truck. As he removed the gas cap he did not want to look at the men for fear they were watching him. "Not gonna look, I am NOT going to look," he thought. Then, he glanced at the side view mirror and met eyes with the driver.

"He knows," Richie said to Mooj. Mooj gave him a grave look.

"We're out in the middle of nowhere. If he calls the cops we're like fish in a barrel."

Joe stood by the truck trying to act as if nothing was going on. He could see the two men talking. Too old to run and definitely too old to fight them, playing it cool was his best option; or so he thought.

"Forty one dollars even," Joe told the driver.

"You got cold drinks inside?"

"Yes sir."

Mooj put his hand on Ritchie's arm.

"I'll go."

"My partners gotta break a fifty anyway," Richie told

Indian Joe.

"Come on, show me where they are," Mooj told him, taking the old man by the arm. A feeling of dread came over Joe as he looked at Richie who could only look away as Mooj led the old man inside.

Bustamante cruised east on the highway still looking for the minivan. They couldn't have come this far he thought as he slowed to make a u-turn. Not in that minivan. Bustamante's car was put together specifically for cruising long hot roads at very high speeds. The green minivan with its hardware to accommodate a baby seat and numerous cup holders was not. Bustamante headed west keeping an eye out for the minivan trying some off road maneuvers.

CHAPTER 27

THE END OF THE LINE FOR INDIAN JOE

Longway, Arizona

Richie drove the green pickup truck down the highway scanning the mirrors and dashboard trying to familiarize himself with the knobs and buttons on the fly. It was refreshing not to be driving a stolen vehicle. He looked over at Mooj who was studying a map.

"I have to say that was pretty smooth."

"It was. But we're not out of the woods yet," Mooj said trying to orient the map by turning it to the left, then to the right.

Richie could see in the bed of the pickup truck two large red gas cans they'd acquired from Indian Joe's. He could hear the two Styrofoam chests filled with ice squeaking against each other.

Richie watched the desert as it passed by slowly despite their speed.

"Hand me a root beer will ya?"

Indian Joe grabbed a root beer from the cooler and opened it. Richie noticed the concern on his face. Indian Joe had told them the police were on to them. He also told them they were looking for them in the minivan. The pickup truck they were in would probably be good for a short while.

"Indian Joe, how old are you?"

"Eighty three," the old man told him.

"How did you get to live to be eighty three?"

"By minding my own damn business," he said firmly.

Silence fell over the truck except for the whirring of the tires. Mooj glanced over to Richie and went back to looking over his map.

"Jesus Christ! They are going to kill me and leave me in the desert. I am a fucking GONER," Indian Joe thought as he scanned the road for any sign of Bustamante in his highway patrol car.

"How many miles to the border?"

"Too many," Mooj told Richie. Indian Joe sat in the rear seat looking helpless.

"I figure now is as good as place as any," Richie announced.

Joe swallowed hard; his heart pounded even harder.

"Hey guys. I have bad eyesight. Some people think I am crazy. Even if I did talk to the cops, they probably wouldn't believe anything I told them." Richie pulled to the side of the road. Mooj looked over to Richie then to Indian Joe.

"Want me to take care of him?"

Richie nodded solemnly.

Mooj climbed out of the passenger side of the extended cab pickup and opened the rear passenger side door.

"End of the line, old timer."

Indian Joe looked at Richie who looked straight ahead.

"Come on we haven't got all day."

Indian Joe slid out of the truck and his feet hit the pavement.

Mooj reached back inside.

"Probably getting the gun," Joe thought.

He scanned the area. A cluster of jagged shrubs about forty yards away might be a good hiding spot if he could only run. He looked at Mooj; young, in shape, mentally sharp from what he could see. Indian Joe resigned himself to the fact that there was no escape. His time had come.

Mooj pulled one of the coolers out of the truck and placed it on the ground. He threw a hand towel in the ice and a few cans.

"This will keep you going for a while. Someone will be by no doubt." Mooj grabbed a baseball cap from inside and put it on the old man's head.

"If you get too hot just put the towel on your head. Dip it in the ice water first."

Joe held his chest.

"Thank you. Oh Jesus, thank you."

"I hate to leave you out here but we're in a bind."

"No problem. No problem at all."

Mooj reached in his pocket and striped off eight one hundred dollar bills and tucked them in the pocket of the old man's shirt.

"That's for the gas and drinks and whatever else you can do for us."

Mooj slapped the old man on the shoulder and jumped back in the truck then stuck his head out the window and yelled.

"Remember, you are deaf dumb and blind!"

"Yes sir," the old Indian said hoisting a big thumbs up.

As the pickup truck sped away Indian Joe looked in the cooler and picked up a cold can marked root beer. He dropped it back in and grabbed another, also a root beer. He pushed the ice back and forth and spotted one.

"Beer," he said tearing the pop top open.

"Thank you Lord! Thank YOU Lord!"

CHAPTER 28

CACTUS CLASH

Frustrated, Officer Bustamante sped down the highway looking for anything that moved. Four wanted men had slipped through his fingers and he was determined catch them. As he sped down the road he came up on a gray Dodge pickup truck; heavy duty type. He swung to the left to pass the truck and while passing, looked to his right.

"Son of a bitch," Bustamante blurted out. He recognized the driver immediately and saw the barrel of an M-4 being raised by the man in the passenger seat. Bustamante slammed on his brakes causing the Dodge to fly past him.

A divot about the size of a half dollar magically appeared on his windshield just under the rear view mirror. Suddenly three more divots penetrated the windshield and warm air was more noticeable as it rushed in. Bustamante grabbed his microphone. The grey Dodge slammed on its brakes and Bustamante's car slammed into the rear setting off the air bag and cutting off the engine.

The Dodge accelerated twenty feet and then stopped.

Bustamante could see the hood of his car had buckled upward and the back of the truck was heavily damage. The armed passenger was climbing out hurriedly. He was big, muscular.

As James lay across the seat he grabbed his M-4 and pushed the muzzle over the dash board. Eight rounds from an automatic rifle ripped into the headrest and cage of his vehicle discouraged him from popping his head up. He fired blindly toward the source of the gunfire, as best as he could tell. Quickly he opened the driver door and slithered out onto the roadway and noticed the driver of the Dodge getting out with a handgun. Bustamante fired and watched the man try to dodge bullets. He had, then ran to the front of the truck and fired back at Bustamante striking the roadway. Looking down, Bustamante grimaced when he saw a round had entered his torso just under his vest. He got low and moved to rear of his patrol car trying to prevent either of the two men from approaching him.

Dave knelt on one knee, his muscles burning from tearing open the stitches he had gotten in his first bullet wound. A new wound was about two inches above the first one. He felt as though the air had been let out of him.

"Partner! Moving to your position!"

"Move," the driver told him as he covered down on the wrecked police car and wounded officer taking cover behind it.

"Arizona Charlie David Ocean seven four two! Grey Dodge pickup truck! Shots fired," Bustamante yelled into his microphone with no answer. Taking a deep breath he lay on the ground and could see two pair of boots, one tan, the other black, in front of the Dodge. Bustamante reached for his radio on his belt. He found the on off switch and turned it on.

"Could be why no one was answering me," he thought.

"Shirley, shots fired on Route sixty eight, two gunmen in a grey Dodge, Arizona license plate Charlie David Ocean seven four two. My cars wrecked and I'm hit. I'm gonna need some help."

Shirley sat at the dispatch console and heard several officers trying to report they were on the way. She said nothing. It wasn't any use.

"Eight miles east of Indian Joe's Gas."

A jumbled mess of radio transmissions was heard. James Bustamante lay on the ground on his stomach with his M-4 rifle sideways, trying to line up a shot when he heard someone coming his way from behind.

"Thank God," he thought as he kept his eyes on the feet of the two gunmen. A pickup truck pulled up alongside of him and he glanced up. The brown one from the van was now in a green pickup truck looking down at him. The green pickup truck sped forward and turned in front of the damaged grey Dodge.

"Now I got them," the policeman thought. As the two gunmen ran toward the green pickup Bustamante rolled from behind the police cruiser and lined up his sights only to notice three men were lining their sights up on him. He rolled back behind the car and instantaneously a barrage of clanging and banging erupted all around him and pieces of his police car bent, broke and shattered. He could hear the green pickup truck speed away with all four occupants but waited a few seconds to make sure he was alone. Putting his hand to his waist he felt blood; lots of it.

CHAPTER 29

SKELETON CREW HEADIN' EAST!

Phoenix, Arizona

Rich opened the door of the hotel room and dropped his two large duffel bags on the floor. He pulled the covers down on one of the beds and gave a thumb up from the door. Mooj supported Dave as he made it from the truck to the hotel room and onto the bed.

"We need some things. Right away," the Driver said.

Taking the top sheet off of the hotel note pad Richie held pen to paper.

"Hydrogen peroxide, neosporine, needle and heavy gauge thread, rubbing alcohol, heavy duty packing tape, gauze pads, ace bandage, box of doughnuts, a pound of coffee and half and half."

"Is that for the patient or for you? "

"All of us."

Finishing up the list he wrote "half and half and almond

milk.”

“I’m going to apply pressure until you get back so don’t take all day,” Mooj told Richie as he picked up the towels from the bathroom and threw them on the bed.

“Use these for the time being.”

Dave lay on the bed and looked at his wounds.

“It doesn’t really hurt much, just—“

“Kinda makes you sick to your stomach,” the driver finished his sentence.

“Yeah. I dislocated my knee years ago and it I almost threw up when I saw it.”

“Been there. I saw a kid rip his front teeth out when he caught them on a chain basketball net coming down from a lay-up,” Mooj chimed in squinting his eyes and covering his front teeth with his hand.

“GOD damn it,” Dave said while the other two laughed covered their mouths, wincing.

“Ahhhh! Shit,” Dave said holding his stomach.

“Don’t make me laugh!”

As Richie left, Mooj began to bring in all of their equipment and cash.

“Mooj, do me a favor, hold this for a few minutes, I have to make a call,” the driver told him.

Mooj dropped the last of the bags and pulled a chair over to the bed.

"Pretty bad luck," Mooj said folding up the wash cloth and placing it on Dave's wound.

"Twice in the same spot," Dave added.

"I should have told Richie to buy me some lottery tickets," Dave said with a smile. Who gets shot twice in one week and lives to tell about it?"

"You do," Mooj reminded him.

The driver walked outside and dialed his cell phone.

"It's me."

"How are you?"

"Did you get the word about Carlos?"

"I did," the man on the phone said.

"One of the others was wounded. The same guy, Dave just caught another one about two hours ago. We had a run in with trooper."

"Sounds like bad luck; do you want to swap him out?"

"No. Not at all. This is a good crew. We got something here."

"I'm listening."

"They work well together, they have a good chemistry. No dopers, drunks, no hot heads. They look at it like legitimate work. They stay in shape, train, even play together well. They're a team. Usually after a job most guys want their cut and have to go somewhere to calm down. These guys all want to find a good steak house. They have a few cocktails;

nice dinner sometimes hit a strip club. We've definitely hit a rough patch but they'll bounce back."

"Good. You need a doctor?"

"I think so."

"What's the closest airport?"

"Phoenix, Arizona."

"All right. I'll have someone meet you there; I'll call you with the details."

"Thanks."

"One more thing, our Vegas crew went off the rails. They got a little too big so our Seattle crew is going to go out and shut them down. We're a little tight right now."

"I understand," the driver told his boss.

"Once you get situated head for Atlantic City. We might have something pretty big for you in that area. I know your man's hurt so take a few weeks to recuperate."

"Atlantic City, understood"

"I'll call you about the doctor."

A few blocks away Rich saw a pharmacy getting ready to close. He entered as a beautiful young woman approached the doors. Black hair, big brown eyes and a sparkling smile, Richie's eyes widened when he saw her.

"Are you closing?"

"We're getting ready to," she said as her manager looked over at her.

"I'm on a road trip with a couple of my friends. One stepped on an old nail earlier. Could I just get these few things? I promise I'll get out of your hair," Richie flashed his best earnest young American male smile at her. She caught it and her heart fluttered.

"Sure. That will be fine. Let me see your list."

Rich handed it to her.

"Strong and masculine," she thought impressed by his height. "Handsome, polite but slightly forceful. Cute. Definitely cute," she thought.

They walked up and down the aisle plucking each item from the list except for the coffee and half and half.

The store manager watched as they flirted with each other and then looked at his watch.

"I have to get coffee and half and half while I am out. Is there a place that is open this late?"

"I'm headed there now," the clerk told him as she began scanning his items.

"Would you like to follow me?"

CHAPTER 30

I.A. SHOWDOWN

Greenlee N.J.

Sergeant Morrow sat with Chief Wilson and Detective Fritz. The Chief seemed serious. He wasn't sure why Fritz was in the room but wondered if it was in case the conversation led to another internal affairs investigation.

"We really haven't come up with much on the Tiki Bar fight. Everyone is pretty tight lipped."

Morrow jumped slightly when Captain Fertid cleared his throat after walking up behind Morrow's seat.

"Nervous?"

Fertid smiled at Morrow.

"Did you send Bogard to interview the wrestler like I asked you?"

"Well, no. He wasn't available," Morrow lied boldly to the Chief.

Knowing the wrestler would immediately recognize Bogard, it was not possible to obey the Chief's order; not if he wanted to keep his job.

The Chief's phone rang. Fertid moved to the window and sat on the small typewriter desk there. He seemed amused.

"Please let it be some sort of gruesome crime," Morrow thought, hoping to divert the spot light onto something else.

Wilson nodded and gave a quick "mmm hmmm".

He picked up his pen then didn't write. Morrow watched hoping a new adventure would let the Tiki Bar fight slide into local history, unsolved.

"Detective Fritz is here with me. I'll send him down."

Fritz perked up.

"The custodian at the Circus found a handgun on the dance floor.

The Chief threw his pen on the desk in disgust.

"Do you think it may be Leoni's," Morrow asked.

"It sounds like it is. I hope not. Leoni will have a lot of explaining to do. He was emphatic that he doesn't take his gun with him when he goes to bars."

Detective Fritz rose and picked up his portable radio and keys.

"I'll let you know if it is his as soon as I find out."

"You sound like you have more important things brewing Chief. I'll come back later," Morrow said as he flew out of his chair and toward the door.

"Hold it right there," the Chief barked.

"Yes sir?"

Detective Fritz smiled as he walked out of the office. Captain Fertid sat with his arms folded and a smug look on his face.

"Do you have any sins you want to confess," the Chief asked referring to the Tiki Bar fight from night court.

Morrow's heart pounded.

"Does the Chief know about the stolen gun? Or is he talking about the Tiki Bar fight?"

Presenting his best innocent face, he asked the Chief

"What do you mean?"

"Why the hell do I get myself in these situations? How do I always end up wondering if the other shoe is going to drop?"

"Nothng Sergeant, just messing with your mind. All in fun," Wilson said as he shooed Morrow out of his office. Morrow walked out shaken.

CHAPTER 31

DETECTIVE FRITZ VS. FRANK

Detective Fritz walked into the Circus Tavern and noticed how different it looked during daylight hours. Ed Crilley was busy counting numerous stacks of money behind the bar when he saw Fritz.

"Frank," Ed yelled.

"The police are here!"

Frank greeted Detective Fritz and walked him to the dance floor in the banquet room. He pointed to a table in the corner.

"Under there. I didn't want to touch it."

Fritz grabbed the pistol and pulled the slide back slightly to see if it was loaded. It was. He looked at the serial number and compared it to the one he had written down on his steno pad.

"Give me one second," Fritz said to Frank as he texted the

Chief's cell phone:

"Leoni's gun is recovered."

"Good," was the chief's reply.

Fritz asked the custodian to have a seat and turned to a new sheet on his steno pad.

"Can you tell me what happened?"

Frank leaned forward in his chair and clasped his hands together.

"Well I was sweeping up. I generally push all the tables to one side and sweep and then I push everything the other way and sweep the other side."

Fritz made a few chicken scratches on his pad.

"How often do you do this?"

"Well I sweep everyday but I usually only push all of the tables from side to side twice a week."

"So this gun has been here for three or four days," Fritz mused.

"What kind of idiot drops his gun in a nightclub?"

"One of our idiots, on the department," Fritz told him.

"Oh, I 'm sorry. I didn't mean to imply…"

"No, you're right. He is an idiot," the Detective said waiving his hand brushing aside the remark.

"It was reported missing a few days ago."

"Is that how long it's been missing?"

"Yes," Fritz said curtly.

"I'm not sure how you missed it for four days," Fritz said with an accusatory tone.

"Hmmm. That *is* strange."

Frank sat back in his chair and cocked an eyebrow. Detective Fritz noticed the change in the custodians' demeanor and decided to pressure him. He ceremoniously turned over a new page on his steno pad, dropped his pen and pad on the table, stood and took off his jacket. The custodian watched every mannerism closely.

"Is this going to take long," he asked the Detective.

"Nah. Just a minute or two," Fritz lied.

"Let me ask you this. Do you know any of our officers personally? Are you friends with any of them? Or, are you related to any of them," Fritz asked with a firm tone.

Frank cleared his throat, his eyes swept back and forth.

"Well, yeah. Sergeant Morrow is my cousin."

"Ser-geant Morrow," Fritz repeated almost singing his name.

"Yes."

Frank knew he had given up a valuable clue to the Detective but didn't want to tip his hand and show he was concerned.

"Anyone else," Fritz asked almost daring him to continue.

"I know a few of the guys just from coming in here," he admitted feeling like he was giving up way too much information.

"It's a small town, probably everyone here knows a few of the officers," he continued.

"True," Fritz said almost completely brushing off the remark while he furiously wrote on his pad. Frank tried to nonchalantly look over the top of the pad to see what Fritz was writing.

"Frank," Fritz started "do you know that I am conducting an internal affairs investigation?"

"No. I thought you were following up on a lost or stolen gun."

"I am. Before we go any further, let me read you your Miranda warning. Just as a matter of procedure, I'm not accusing you of anything."

Frank folded his arms. Fritz looked at his laminated Miranda card.

"Before I read this, I just want you to know that if you are withholding any information or lying, it is a criminal offense."

Frank did his best to conceal the sheer terror that overcame him.

"Not that I suspect you," he lied "but if someone did steal one of the departments firearms it is obviously a very serious matter."

"Of course," Frank said his voice trailing off.

"Let me read this to you and then I will wrap this up."

"You have the right to remain silent…"

CHAPTER 32

IA Target : Sergeant Morrow

Detective Fritz sat at his desk and shuffled papers while Captain Fertid stood with his hands in his pockets looking out the window.

Morrow walked in.

"You wanted to see me?"

Fritz gestured to the chair across the desk from him.

Morrow sat down with an inquisitive look on his face.

"What's this about?"

Fritz slid a few forms across the desk and Morrow picked them up.

"Internal affairs investigation? Me?"

"Read them carefully and then let me know if you think you need a union representative or a lawyer."

Fritz chose his words carefully creating an impression that if Morrow did want either, it was an indication of guilt.

"I don't think I do," Morrow said casually.

He looked over the forms and signed them with what appeared to be clean conscience. He looked them over and slid them back to Fritz.

"I'm curious. What is this about?"

"Leoni's stolen gun," Fritz barked.

"Holy shit!" Morrow thought,

"It was stolen," he asked.

Fritz sat back calmly and pulled out his steno pad and paged through his notes.

"Leoni's gun was found on the floor of the Circus Tavern by one of the custodians."

"And?"

"Care to guess which one?"

Morrow shrugged his shoulders.

"Your cousin. Frank."

"O.K. …and that involves me… how?"

Fritz looked him square in the eye.

"Frank told me everything. Connolly took Leoni's gun and you asked him to report it found in the bar."

"Why would I do that?"

"To make Leoni look like an idiot!"

"He does a good enough job of that by himself."

"I know you, well, *most* people know he is Council Frost's

tit man but this is underhanded!"

Morrow sat back in his chair and smiled.

"You're bluffing!"

"When was the last time you spoke to Frank?"

Morrow cocked his head and his eyes darted to the right.

"Probably at my aunt's Christmas party."

"Are you sure?"

"Pretty sure, yeah."

"You do know what the penalties are for lying don't you?"

"Do you know what the penalties are for calling me a liar?"

"Are you threatening me?"

Morrow shot up out of his chair and pointed his finger at Fritz.

"No! You're threatening me! Listen to me! …"

Captain Fertid grabbed Morrow by the arm.

Detective Fritz rose from his chair and threw his pen down.

Fertid held his hand up.

"Hold on for a minute. Sergeant Morrow, here's a quick fix. Let me take a look at your cell phone. The Chief will ask if we looked at it. If you didn't talk to or text Frank we can assume you didn't have anything to do with it."

Morrow looked at his cell phone and his eyes widened.

CHAPTER 33

JOHNNY LEE ARREST

Two o'clock in the morning at the Circus Tavern was not for faint of heart. Hard core drinkers, horny, past their prime ladies and well sauced men sat at the bar trying to decide which pleasure was worth pursuing. Big John walked in and immediately saw Johnny Lee perched at the end of the bar talking with two hags around the corner from him. Hags, or swamp donkeys as he liked to call them, littered the bar on both sides.

"Shots all around," he yelled to the bartender.

The woman sitting next to him looked at him as if her prayers had been answered.

"What's the occasion hon," she asked putting her hand on Big John's arm. He wanted to pull it off but didn't.

"A good night at the casino for a change," he told her with most people at the bar listening in. Johnny Lee leaned in.

"You hit it big?"

Big John nodded.

"I can't quit my day job but I'm gonna get tanked tonight!"

"What's your pleasure," the bartender asked.

"Tequila for me."

Several shouts of "tequila" and a "fuck yeah" were directed at the bartender who lined up the shot glasses and poured. Big John threw a hundred dollar bill on the bar and raised his glass.

"To one armed bandits!" Everyone followed suit downing the shot.

"Set 'em up again," Big John ordered. The bartender began refilling everyone's shot glasses.

As time went on Big John began to notice some things. The swamp donkey sitting next to him wasn't what he had first thought. Her leopard skin tights accentuated her shapeless legs and boney ass. Her bright red prostitute lipstick was looking quite playful now. Johnny Lee was still sitting at the corner talking to two not so young ladies. Several shots later Lee was still looking fresh. Big John checked himself out in the reflection of his cell phone. He could see the bags under his eyes sagging, his hair was askew and his eyes were having trouble working together.

"One more round of shots," he yelled. The liquored up group cheered and, once refilled, hoisted them up in honor of John and his victory over the one armed bandits.

"What are ya doin' tonight hon," the woman next to him said as she causally brushed the back of her hand on his groin.

He looked at her. Despite copious amounts of alcohol and a wild imagination, she was definitely out of his league. At least fifteen years older than him, she seemed to be melting before his very eyes. She smiled at him and, while glancing over her shoulder, Big John noticed Johnny Lee was gone. His glass and a few dollars left as a tip were pushed up to the inside of the bar.

"Shit! Gotta go," he said, grabbing his jacket as he stormed out.

Sergeant Morrow sat in his truck and scanned the street with binoculars. He was uncomfortable watching the neighborhood in the dark in plain clothes. He knew Johnny Lee wasn't on the move yet. He would have heard from Big John. He sat quietly and ran scenarios through his head envisioning several ways the stakeout could pan out; a foot chase, through the neighbors yards. Who has a dog? Who has a fence? Who has a clothesline? No one in this day and age he guessed. Surely he wouldn't be armed. What if he was? How would Bogard do? Every indication was that he could take care of himself. He was quick, a good shot. Morrow had seen him use his flashlight on a car stop when a drunk tried to wrestle him to the ground. One solid, swift blow to the noggin ended the affair. But Bogards real talent? He could run. Being about a dozen years younger than he and Connolly, Bogard would be the top dog in a show of speed; but for pure might, Big John all the way.

"Ping," erupted from Morrow's phone. A text message read

"J Lee on the move. Lost him. Look out."

Morrow could see that the text was sent to Bob Connolly too. Not to cause any undue noise, Morrow sat quietly in the truck knowing that Connolly and Bogard were ready, hiding in the bushes next door to Lee's house, waiting for the first signs of nocturnal burglar.

Bogard had finally gotten warm by curling up in the cluster of bushes and drifted off to sleep. Connolly was still sitting upright. His mouth was open and his head slightly cocked. He still had binoculars in hand but he was just as asleep as his partner.

Morrow was the only one awake, but the humming of the engine and the warm air were pulling his eyelids down.

Big John trotted slowly toward the baseball field and listened for Johnny Lee. From time to time he could hear brisk footsteps and panting. He suspected it was from the overweight burglar. As he moved through the night he was surprised at the stillness.

Prowling the neighborhood he heard glass break. He ran toward the sound. He searched the homes in the immediate area looking for broken windows and tried his best not to make a sound. His eye caught a quick flash of light across the street. A flashlight inside a house perhaps? As he moved toward the house, he could see a small window on the side door was broken and where the thief had apparently reached inside and unlocked the door. Big John moved inside, his pistol drawn. He shined his flashlight around the dining room of the small house. He could see on the hutch cabinet rings in the dust where round objects had been sitting; candle sticks maybe. Some sort of vase? As he looked at the hutch, through the window he caught the glimpse of the portly burglar climbing over the fence in the rear yard.

Big John grabbed his radio and made sure he was on channel two.

"Johnny Lee is headed toward the ball field carrying a sack. It looks like he broke into a house on Utley Place. I'm here now. I'm going to try to follow him."

Morrow sat in his truck, mouth hanging wide open oblivious to the radio traffic. Connolly and Bogard were in the same state of unconsciousness.

"Morrow, do you read me?"

John ran from the house and tried to scale the fence as Johnny Lee had. Perhaps it was the booze, perhaps it was his weight, or just maybe it was his shoes, but Big John could not get over the fence. After two feeble attempts, he decided to go around the block and intercept the suspect. As he made it to the corner, he could see Johnny Lee scampering across the baseball field. John hurried but was his progress was slow. As he watched the burglar disappear into the neighborhood on the other side of the baseball field, he quickened his pace, but the stabbing in his right kidney area made him stop. Queasiness had set in. The tequila shots didn't help nor did the mozzarella sticks he had eaten at the bar… or the loaded potato skins. Perhaps it was the stuffed mushrooms. John slowed to a walk and tried the radio again.

"Morrow, do you read me?"

Nothing. Big John wandered the neighborhood and stopped for a breather. He bent over, placed his hands on his knees and drew in a deep breath. Then about thirty feet away, he heard the front door open from a darkened house and looked up. Johnny Lee stepped out gingerly and quietly closed the door behind him. As he turned around the two men saw each other.

"Cock sucker," Big John yelled as he gave chase. Johnny Lee hoisted the pillow case filled with stolen goods and swung it at Big John and the contents spilled onto the yard. Johnny Lee ran. Big John chased him. The further they ran the further back Big John fell. When he noticed Morrows truck sitting on the side of the street he smacked the driver window and yelled "Come on!" Morrow woke in a panic, saw the two fat men running down the street and laid on his horn.

Connolly continued to sleep and Bogard woke up just in time to see Johnny Lee run by the cluster of bushes toward his house. Bogard sprang from the bushes and gave chase. Big John again succumbed to the stabbing pain in his side and the queasy feeling in his stomach. He watched as Bogard sprinted to catch Johnny Lee and tried to tackle him. Instead, Lee kept running with the younger lighter Bogard riding on his back. Bogard covered Lee's eyes with one hand.

"You're under arrest, motherfucker!"

Johnny Lee kept moving to his front porch and slowly up the steps. He grabbed the hand rail and tried to pull himself up while Bogard continued to cover his face and wrestle him off the porch. As Morrow approached he noticed how Bogard looked like a child getting a piggy back ride from his dad.

Morrow passed Big John and almost tripped over Connolly who was crawling out of the bushes. On the porch Morrow grabbed Johnny Lee around the waist, Lee opened the storm door but it was immediately slammed shut by Bogard who was reaching over Lee's shoulder. Connolly ran up the steps and grabbed on to Lee who fought to free himself from the group, shattering the glass storm door when the gang of men fell into it.

"Get off me! Get off me," Johnny Lee shouted as he thrashed about trying to shake the three plainclothes officers.

"You're under arrest mother fucker," Bogard shouted, his legs still dangling in the air as he clung to the suspects' neck.

As Big John approached he could hear himself wheezing and gasping for air. The sharp pain under his ribs was getting worse. He could see the melee' on Johnny Lee's porch and tried to run toward it. He pulled himself up the three steps and reached into the group, planted his feet and swung Johnny Lee and everyone attached to the ground. As the group of men swarmed on their man, Bogard was able to handcuff one arm but Johnny Lee had the other arm under him. Big John strained to pull it out, and the tequila shots, stuffed mushrooms, loaded potato skins and fried mozzarella sticks worked their way up his esophagus and onto the group under him. The bulk of the discharge landed on Johnny Lee.

"What the fuck?!!! What the fuck," Lee squealed. Connolly started gagging immediately and withdrew. Morrow began wiping his contaminated sleeve on the burglar. As Lee struggled, he was overcome and finally submitted to the arrest.

In the treatment stall in the emergency room, Big John sat on the bed next to Johnny Lee. He had vomit on his shirt and pants, his eyes were still red and watery. His faded blue jeans had mud on the knees and grass stains on the seat and thighs as well as the elbows of his jacket. He reeked of booze.

Johnny Lee was in slightly worse shape. Being on the bottom of the pig pile he had some scrapes and bruises from hitting the sidewalk and falling into the bushes. A few slivers of glass had worked their way into his skin on his left hand and wrist. A fat lip and a skinned eyebrow completed the ensemble.

Morrow, Bogard and Connolly stood in the door way watching Johnny Lee as he tried to explain why he ran.

"I didn't know who you were," he said to Big John.

"Bull-SHIT," Big John countered.

"Seriously, I had no idea."

"I've been a cop for almost twenty years in this town and you don't know who I am? I find that hard to believe."

"Look at you. You don't look much like a cop right now. None of you guys do."

A middle aged nurse approached the door way, abruptly burst out with an "Ex-CUSE me!"

Morrow moved out of her way and she gave him a condescending look as she entered.

"What's this? The whole family came down with you?"

She looked at the men with disdain and put on a new pair of bright purple rubber gloves.

"What's your main complaint?"

"These officers jumped on me and beat me, for no reason! They all piled on."

The nurse looked at Connolly and Morrow.

"Did you beat this man for no reason?"

"No ma'am, we beat him for a good reason. Now if you don't mind patch him up so we can get him out of here and get on with our investigation."

The nurse started to clean the scrapes on Johnny Lee's face and she looked over at Big John.

"What's your story?"

"I was born a poor young black child in the back woods of Arkansas."

"Hey smart ass, I mean what injuries do you have?"

"Pulled groin. Can you rub some pain relieving gel on it?"

The nurse looked at Big John, at his vomit, his dirty stained clothing.

She looked at Morrow.

"Why isn't this prisoner handcuffed?"

Morrow looked at her sheepishly.

"He is actually a police officer."

"This guy here with the vomit and the mud and the foul mouth."

"Yes ma'am."

"Hard to believe sometimes," Connolly chimed in.

"Well his color is bad. We'll have to catheterize him, collect his urine and analyze it."

Big John slid off of the bed.

"I'll wait in the car."

"Good idea," the nurse said as she watched him leave.

CHAPTER 34

THE STATION

Bogard picked up a small fancy cardboard box from a basket already labeled with a case number. Connolly sat next to him at a computer typing. Bogard opened the box and removed eight forks and placed them evenly across the desk and took a picture of them.

"Eight sterling silver salad forks."

"How do you know they are sterling silver salad forks," Connolly asked.

"It says so right here," Bogard said turning over one of the forks showing Connolly the imprint: "Sterling silver."

"No. I mean how do you know it's a salad fork?"

"It's shorter that the regular dinner fork," Bogard said smugly.

"Actually it's a pie fork," Big John said from the corner, having awoken from his short nap.

"A pie fork? Who are you trying to kid?"

"The pie fork is shorter than the dinner fork and wider than the salad fork. Were you guys raised in the wild?"

Connolly looked at the disgusting mess Big John had become.

"It's hard to take etiquette advice from someone who recently vomited upon themselves and *still* bears the noodles on his shirt," Connolly told him.

"How about taking etiquette advice from someone while they HAVE THEIR FOOT UP YOUR ASS?"

"Girls! Girls! Girls," Morrow said as he entered the room.

Fertid walked in wearing blue jeans and a red t-shirt. He handed Morrow a copy of the affidavit and search warrant.

"These copies are for the case file. Oh, by the way, I just got done talking to the Chief."

Everyone looked at him expecting him to pass on what was sure to be many accolades for solving numerous burglaries. Even Big John sat up straight.

"Did you know that Johnny Lee is the Chief's cousin?"

"The same Johnny Lee that we just tackled, threw down the steps and choked and crushed half to death," Morrow asked.

"Our Johnny Lee is the Chiefs' cousin?"

"He is," Fertid told them.

"Is he pissed?"

Fertid took a deep breath and sat down in a desk chair.

He balled up his right hand into a fist.

"Not sure," he said slowly as he exhaled.

"He isn't easy to read sometimes."

Connolly and Bogard exchanged a worried look.

CHAPTER 35

ROUTE 40 EAST DIVERSION

"Delaware Memorial Bridge" the sign read. The men were glad to see it. It had been an adventurous road trip and they were glad to see it end, if only for a while. As they approached the bridge Richie handed the toll money to the toll booth attendant. Dave lay across the back of their latest van. He still complained every time Richie hit a bump in the road or took a turn too suddenly. Mooj was sound asleep. The driver, despite his nickname, was navigating. His collection of maps was neatly tucked away in a brown cardboard file folder. He excelled at navigating. He would open cans, peel wrappers off of food, count change for tolls for whomever was driving. He could give turn by turn directions as good as any navigation system. Looking over the side of the bridge he saw many boats in the water and thought how refreshing it looked.

"Once we get settled," the driver said "I think we ought to rent a boat, maybe go on a fishing trip or something. We're going to have a few weeks to kill."

Dave, still holding his wound, shook his head.

"How about a Pilates class too?"

As they headed down the bridge into New Jersey, Dave told Richie

"Look for Route 40 East, once you are on that stay on it until we start seeing signs for Atlantic City."

"O.K., I can handle that."

The driver sat back and reclined his seat.

"I'm going to take a nap. Wake me up if anything good happens."

He waited about thirty seconds.

"Route 40 east. Want me to jot it down for you?"

"I'm good," Richie told him.

"Route 40 East."

Richie took the van through the small, old town of Lower Alloway Creek and through Salem New Jersey. Brick buildings, historical markers in front of homes and the beautiful green pastures and livestock littered the country side. A large green field was dotted with ducks and ducklings that ran through the cows and bulls.

"I could hang out in a place like this."

"Yup," was the drivers' only reply, cracking his eyes open for just a second. Mooj and Dave didn't stir. As dusk turned to darkness Richie could feel the tension slipping away. The van wandered through the town onto a two lane highway with light traffic Richie noticed what appeared to be a rather impressive but desolate toll booth. As he pulled up, a big man, maybe three hundred pounds wearing the most gear he had ever seen on a human being emerged from inside the booth.

A scornful look adorned his face. The man wore BDU pants, a dark polo shirt and combat boots. He was heavily armed.

"Can I help you?"

Richie looked at his rifle slung across his chest. He also wore a handgun, radios, gas mask and extra magazines and handcuffs. His tactical vest was adorned with several Velcro pouches, straps and brass snaps that it was impossible to tell what they were all for.

"I think I am lost," Richie told the man. He looked at the driver who was sound asleep.

"You sure you're not gunrunners trying to come in here and tear up our operation?"

Richie looked at the armed man. He didn't crack a smile; he stood stoically next to the van when suddenly the passenger side of the minivan lit up. Another armed man was on the passenger side shining his light inside. The driver woke up and put his hands on the dashboard.

"I'm a thinkin' we got ourselves a whole van full of gun runners."

Richie thought about the collection of automatic weapons in the cargo area of the van; pistols, rifles, flash bang grenades and enough ammunition for a small war, not to mention the cash; plenty of cash.

Richie wondered who these men were and if they could be bribed.

Mooj looked from the back seat at Richie. All three knew the other men had the drop on them. Although they weren't covering down on them, they knew they were out gunned, out maneuvered. Richie thought about the pistol tucked between his seat and the console. He might be able to get the man closest to him but his partner would undoubtedly riddle the van once gun fire erupted. The driver sat there with his hands on the dashboard and looked at Richie and shook his head back and forth. He had a grim look on his face.

Finally, the armed man cracked a smile.

"I'm just screwin' with you man," the guard said laughing.

"We don't get too many visitors here. I get a little squirrelly when someone does come by. Where you headed?"

"Atlantic City area," Richie said nervously.

"Hey Dean, what's the best way to get to Atlantic City from here?"

The other guard walked around to the driver's side of the van.

"Just go back the way you came and in about four miles you'll see signs for route 40 east. It'll take you right there."

"I appreciate it, thanks," Richie said putting his van in gear.

The guard slapped Richie's shoulder with his huge paw.

"What is this place anyway?"

"Nu-klur plant," the guard said pointing the way for the u-turn.

"Keep it real man."

"Will do," Richie told him.

Richie swung the van around and waived to the two guards as he drove by. He glanced at the driver who was glared at him.

"Want me to stop somewhere so you can change your underwear," Richie asked smiling.

"Route-forty-EAST."

"Route 40 east. Yes sir. Got it."

CHAPTER 36

RICHIE'S MOM TAKES A RIDE

Santee, California

Regina took her car keys from her tidy little purse and walked out of the front door of her home, locking it. She got into her eighteen year old Chevrolet and backed cautiously down the driveway. Checking her rearview mirror she pulled onto the street. She wondered about Richie. How was he doing? Where was he? It was always nice to hear from him but she worried when he didn't call for more than a week. He *was* doing dangerous work.

As she cruised the local roads she prepared herself for the highway traffic. People were so impatient, whizzing by her at such high speeds. Why was everyone in such a rush these days? She was still sharp as far as women in their early sixties go but definitely not up to speed for highway driving. She clenched the steering wheel, took a deep breath and punched the gas.

She speed along the roadway and counted the familiar signs. The Chicken Shack where they had spent so many

Wednesday nights for dinner. Rosie's Bowling Lanes where she and her husband had competed in so many tournaments. Their first place trophy and photograph were still in the vestibule trophy case from nineteen eighty-eight. Then she saw it; Art's Furniture and Lighting. Art was a dear old friend. He had known Regina and her husband for years, and Richie all of his life. Cub Scout den leader, little league coach, swimming instructor, Art was as dear a friend as a person could hope to have. She loved to do business with him. His furniture was smart, upbeat and durable. Regina didn't like the throw away furniture of nowadays. She still had the same sofa in her living room since the early days of their marriage.

She parked in front of the store and looked through the window and saw Art finishing up with a customer; a lamp, and a nice one at that. As she approached the door she held it for the woman carrying her new lamp outside. She couldn't resist complimenting her on the purchase.

"That is a beautiful lamp," she told the woman.

"Do you think so?

"Oh I know so," she gushed.

"Oh, thank you! I just had to have it," the other woman confessed as she smiled and walked away.

Art met her at the door.

"Regina," he said.

"Just in time. That order you placed has finally come in," he told her holding the door.

"Oh good heavens, I had almost forgotten about it."

They walked to a particularly nice living room set. It was made of brown leather and was matched with wooden coffee table trimmed in the same leather.

"Have a seat and I'll bring it out, look it over and make sure it isn't damaged."

Art walked off and Regina sat on the sofa watching customers, many of them couples as they tried out the various sofas, chairs and kitchen sets throughout the store. She remembered how excited she and her husband were so many years ago furnishing their first apartment together.

"Exciting times," she thought.

Art walked from the back of the store with a cardboard box.

"Let's just make sure it is what you wanted."

Art opened the box and removed the crude looking, short, wide statue of three men with their arms locked at the elbows protecting a sphere which looked like a ball of mud slapped together by a first grader.

Art looked at it.

"*This* is what you ordered?"

"Oh yes. Isn't it magnificent?"

Art looked at the woman he had known for so many years.

"Perhaps she has begun to lose her mind," he thought wondering how he could pull off this whopper of a lie he'd have to tell.

"Unique," he said.

"It's a Francois Dupah," Regina said proudly.

Art nodded wondering who Francois Dupah was, and why he'd do such a terrible thing to mud.

Regina rubbed her hand along the solid ball and admired the piece. She looked at the three mud men circling the outside and ran her fingers over their faces.

"It's not for me, it is actually a gift."

"Not for me I hope," Art thought shuddering at the thought.

"You are always so thoughtful," he said still a bit confused.

"Wrap it up please and I'll take it with me."

With a small wave of the hand Art beckoned a young man of seventeen and promptly and politely asked him to secure it back in the box with bubble wrap to protect it.

Outside the young man carried it to Regina's car and placed it in the trunk. As he turned Regina pulling a five dollar bill out of her purse and handed it to him.

"Oh that's not necessary ma'am,"

"Oh take it. Buy your girlfriend some ice cream or something."

The young man took the tip, thanked Regina and scurried back into the store for his next assignment. Regina got back into her car and prepared to take on the highway.

She worried about her package. She worried that someone

might crash into her and ruin the surprise. As she accelerated she tensed up. Once reaching cruising speed she began to relax a bit. She imagined that if she drove on the highway every day for a week or so she would become accustomed to the pace. She also imagined, quite rightly that she was fooling herself.

None the worse for wear and tear, after a few tense minutes of driving Regina eased off the highway back onto the local roads and finally down her street. She passed her house and admired it as she did. She loved the manicured lawn and bright pink azaleas and the new canvas awnings her husband had installed. It was like a dream cottage and it never looked better.

A few doors down she pulled into the driveway of her neighbor. The once beautiful home had deteriorated into a peeling shack with brown lawn with sporadic weeds growing about the dead grass. It needed a new roof and even the handicap ramp was starting to show its age, but Regina was excited.

Inside, Clay was sitting in his wheelchair his head cocked back, mouth open and his hook dangling from the side of the chair. In what was left of the other hand the remote control for the television was held by a thumb and two fingers. He wore a San Diego Padres baseball jersey with what appeared to be scribbling in black magic marker. He continued to sleep while Regina and her friend Melanie struggled with the cardboard box on the cart as they pushed it up the handicap ramp and inside the door.

Regina looked at Melanie's son.

"How is he doing?"

"Not so good today, maybe tomorrow will be a better day."

Clay sat in the chair still asleep with his head back, looking like he was in pain, but he wasn't. He was numb to everything; pain, food, television, comings and goings of friends and family; everything.

"I can hardly wait to see what this big mystery is," Melanie said.

Regina grabbed the box and Melanie helped her put it on the coffee table.

She opened the box and lifted the monstrosity.

Melanie looked at it, puzzled.

"It needs a little fine tuning. Do you have a hammer?"

Melanie nodded and left to get one.

Clay's sleep was interrupted by his own snoring. His head straightened up and he looked around the room.

Regina smiled at him.

"How are you doing dear?"

Clay just smiled at the familiar, friendly face.

Melanie returned with the hammer.

"Who wrote on his shirt?"

"It's a baseball jersey, all of the San Diego Padres signed it. It came in the mail a few days ago. It was from an old friend the card said."

Regina took the hammer and smashed the statue top. She reached in and pulled out rolls and rolls of cash. Big bills. Lots of really big bills.

"Sweet mother Mary!" Melanie gasped.

"Where'd this come from?"

"From an old friend I guess."

"Whose money is it?"

"Yours."

"Where'd it come from?"

"It did belong to the rotten cocksuckers who sent our boys to war."

"Regina!" Melanie chirped as the two women laughed and leaned into each other.

"One promise you have to make."

"What?"

"No one is to know and it is to take care of Clay and ease the burden on you and Earle. You cannot put this money in the bank."

"This is amazing … it's just that… everything seems to be happening all at once. Last week we had two home health aids show up to give Clay a bath and massage. We thought it was through the Veteran's Administration but it wasn't. These young women show up wearing hospital scrubs and once we get him in the bathtub they close the door. They say we have to be concerned with the patients' modesty. He's in there for about a half hour, forty five minutes and when he comes out he is spic and span from head to toe. It really puts a smile on his face."

Regina smiled a knowing smile.

"Funny thing is, they are all so nice to Clay but," she leaned in and whispered "they are a little tough looking, you know, like hookers or something. But they are awfully sweet."

Regina looked over at Clay.

"How do you like your new health aides?"

Clay smiled and gave her a thumbs up, dropping his remote control.

His head rolled away from her and then back, his smile was even broader.

"When Earle comes home from work we will have a lot to discuss."

CHAPTER 37

CONFRONTATION

Greenlee N.J.

As Morrow and Connolly walked down the hallway of the police station Connolly had a spring in his step. Morrow was much more conscious that someone might be watching. Connolly ducked into the coffee break room which he found empty. Morrow knew to follow him.

"I'm guessing the Chief believed you. Fertid is calling Leoni in to tell him he's being suspended and pulled off the list for the sergeant's exam."

"Fritz couldn't get jack shit from Frank, although I have to admit it was a little hairier than I thought it would be."

"Fritz is no dummy," Connolly added.

"I really didn't expect they'd come after me like that," Morrow said.

"We have to watch our p's and q's."

O'Malley walked in the room and gave both men an

annoyed look and continued toward the coffee pot. Morrow looked him over.

"Is there a problem?"

"No problem Sergeant."

"You look like you got something to say."

O'Malley put the coffee pot down.

He turned slowly and looked at Morrow.

"You know what? I *do* have something to say. I'm kind of pissed off about the deal with Leoni."

"How so?"

"He's getting suspended and he won't be able to take the sergeant's exam. I don't think he did what they accuse him of doing. In fact I believe him when he says someone stole his gun."

"So you think it was planted at the Circus Tavern?"

"I think it is ironic that your cousin found it while sweeping up."

Morrow's heart pounded. Not too many people knew Frank was his cousin.

"You know what makes me even more suspicious? That out of over twenty employees that go in and out of there, your cousin found it."

"So what are you saying? Are you accusing me of something? Internal Affairs have already investigated it."

O'Malley turned around and poured cream into his coffee

and stirred it.

"If it was anyone else, I don't know that I'd have a problem with it. But, there are two things that raise my suspicion."

Morrows face turned serious.

"Go on."

"One, you guys skulk around here like you are up to something all the time. Ever since the Vincelli death you, Connolly and Big John do nothing but huddle in corners and whisper and

watch people. Number two, I've been out with Leoni a bunch of times. He doesn't bring his gun with him when he drinks. We've discussed it. He just won't do it."

Connolly stepped in.

"What are you trying to say?"

"I just said it. Leoni got a raw deal. I think someone set him up."

"Who do you think would do it?" Connolly continued.

"I don't know and I'm not going to guess. It wouldn't be fair unless I actually knew. I hear a lot of rumors about people here" he paused giving Connolly a long look in the eyes.

"I don't assume they are all true."

"I didn't take this job to get involved in office politics or to fuck people out of promotions. I took this job because I wanted to catch criminals."

O'Malley turned his back on Morrow and picked up a plastic lid for his coffee and placed it snugly on his cup.

"Now that I have my coffee I am going to take it with me and get back on the street because that's where the criminals are. Right?"

He looked at Morrow. His face melted into disdain. He left.

Connolly followed him out the door and Morrow called out

"Bob!"

He followed Bob down the hallway and took him by the arm.

O'Malley kept walking unaware that Connolly had been trying to catch up to him.

"That little piss ant!"

"He's right, that's what makes it so hard to swallow," Morrow admitted.

"Fuck him," Connolly blurted out within earshot of O'Malley.

Morrow lowered his voice.

"Bob, how many other people feel the same way about us? I thought we covered our tracks pretty well. Maybe we have to revisit that. We worry so much about covering our asses that we aren't enjoying the job like we used to."

Morrow nodded for Connolly to join him back in the coffee room.

"Do you remember when the state police detectives came in a few weeks back doing the back ground checks?"

Connolly nodded.

"I thought they were here to grab us. I saw them pull up and I thought that was it."

A smile erupted on Connolly's face.

"My stomach turned and my knees began to shake. I was thinking of ways to notify everyone else if they put the arm on me."

"O'Malley is a hundred percent right. Why did you take this job?"

"Yeah I know. But I could still wring his neck for him."

"The truth hurts sometimes," Morrow added.

CHAPTER 38

STRIP CLUB ADVENTURE

Pleasantville N.J.

Richie and the driver pulled into the parking lot of Club Bounce and surveyed the layout. Mooj and Dave were already inside and they agreed not to sit near or acknowledge each other.

"I'm ready for bed," the driver announced.

"That steak dinner finished me off."

Richie shook his head in mock disgust. He started to the front door without even considering not going in.

"Some poor young lady is depending on us to pay her rent. We have an obligation!"

"I suppose."

Richie walked in and was immediately stopped by the bouncer.

"You twenty one?"

Richie said nothing. Instead he handed his California driver's license to the huge, hairless man. The man was trying his best to maintain an air of superiority but Richie towered over him and said nothing.

Reaching behind a small podium, the man whipped out a book listing all of the countries standardized driver's licenses and their anti counterfeit marks and codes. Richie stood calmly as the man looked at the book and then again at the license. He glanced up to gauge Richie's reaction. Richie knew better. He knew it was counterfeit, but he knew it was a good one. Since working with Carlos and the driver, he knew he could depend on whatever documents they provided. He didn't know where they came from except that they were sent to commercial post office boxes and awaited them as they made their way across the country. They were the best.

"You look young for your age," the bouncer told Richie.

"I get that a lot," Richie said with his hand out silently demanding his license back.

Begrudgingly the bouncer handed it back to him.

He wondered why bouncers had such attitudes. They were there to have fun.

The driver entered without being challenged and they took a seat at the bar able to watch Mooj and Dave at their nine o'clock position.

A sweet looking young woman danced on the bar and winked at Richie while the driver looked on. The bartender came over and the driver ordered a beer.

"What'll ya have?"

"Richie," The driver said.

"What do you want?"

Richie never took his eyes off of the woman but was able to gather his thoughts enough to order a rum and coke.

As the music pulsed and the lights dimmed Richie became oblivious to his surroundings and the driver sat back casually and politely tucked cash into each woman's bikini bottom as they paraded by.

It was good to be off the road for a while and enjoy some down time. The driver watched Richie and discreetly watched Mooj and Dave as they played with the girls and drank. Ten days on the road, two shootouts and three robberies showed him this group was tough and disciplined. Their condos in Greenlee provided a nice respite for the men.

Despite two wounds to the abdomen, Dave was still game for go go girls. Suddenly out of the corner of his eye he saw a commotion by Dave. Richie looked over and began to stand up.

"Hold on there," the driver warned him.

"Let it pan out before we get involved."

Richie sat quietly.

The bouncer approached Dave and asked what the trouble was. Dave was doubled over in pain and held his hand up which the bouncer slapped away.

"Hold on," Mooj said to him.

"He's injured."

The manager rushed over and confronted Dave.

"What's your problem?"

The young dancer stood there sheepishly.

"It's my fault."

"What the fuck did you do now?"

Dave looked up at him.

"Hey man, no need to be a dick, it was an accident."

"Don't tell me when to be a dick, what is your fucking problem?"

"I hopped on his lap but he's injured," the woman said.

"I had hernia surgery and I'm a little sore. I'll be alright."

"Oh I am soooo sorry," the woman started.

"God damn it Crystal, why is it always you causing problems?"

Dave stood up and pointed at the manager.

"Hold on a minute."

The bouncer immediately moved in and began to muscle Dave into the bar.

Mooj stepped in between them.

"Just a minute, everybody take a deep breath," he said noticing the bouncer was still leaning on Dave.

"Does he have to pin an injured man against the bar like that?"

The manager waived the goon off.

"We are here to see this beautiful young lady dance. We don't want trouble and we don't want to cause any for you. We just got off a boat and we just got paid and we are looking to drop a lot of cash while we are having a good time. I promise you, we won't cause trouble."

The manager looked as though he was considering it when Mooj pulled out a wad of cash.

"If it is ok with you I would like to buy a drink for everyone at the bar."

Dollar signs rung up in the managers' eyes and he nodded. Dave turned to the woman who had started the commotion.

"I am sorry I got you in trouble with your boss."

"He's a prick. It's always something with him. I'm sorry I jumped up on you like that."

"That's the best thing that has happened to me all week."

She laughed and shoved him lightly.

"Seriously, it's been a shitty week. Are you ladies allowed to drink? Would you like something?"

Down around the corner of the bar the driver watched as the situation resolved itself.

"Nicely done," he thought.

CHAPTER 39

SLIPPING AWAY IN GREENLEE

Greenlee, N.J.

Mooj and the driver walked off the beach across the street toward their condo unit. Mooj hosed off his feet before starting to climb the three flights of wooden stairs to their unit. The driver placed their beach chairs in the small storage shed in the ground floor parking area. He placed the beach badges back on the fabric of the chairs for the next person. As he bounded up the stairs he passed a Pakistani family struggling with two children, a baby and an elderly grandmother. The husband was pulling a plastic wagon with balloon tires filled with beach toys, shovels, buckets and balls. As Mooj came up behind them he took the rear of the wagon and helped the Pakistani man carry it up the steps. The men carried it up the stairs and his wife dragged behind with the brood. The man turned at the third floor and put the wagon down.

"Dank yew, Dank yew," were his only words.

Mooj waved and continued on to the condo and went inside. Dave and Richie sat on the floor wiping down their weapons.

"It's about time," Dave said as he slid his M-4 back into the case.

"You should take a swim in the ocean. It is refreshing. It might improve your disposition," Mooj told him.

"I would if it weren't for these two bullet holes in me."

"And there's nothing wrong with my disposition," Dave said firmly.

"My mistake," Mooj prodded.

"I think I'm going to take a walk. I have to get out for a bit. Maybe hit the stop and rob. Anybody need anything?

"Almond milk," Richie said.

"Doughnuts," the driver added

"Solarcaine," Mooj said.

"You sunburned Mooj? How can you tell," Dave asked.

"Not for me, for him," pointing to the driver.

"Am I sunburned?"

""Not yet, give it an hour. You pink people have very tender skins."

The driver shrugged.

"It couldn't hurt."

"Also a gallon of milk," Mooj added.

"What the fuck?!!!"

Dave threw his arms up.

"If it isn't too much for you... I know your arms are getting pretty scrawny since you haven't been able to work out lately."

"Fuck you; you little Arab," Dave barked.

"I'll get the milk. I'll milk the bull myself!"

Dave grabbed his condo key and checked his pockets for cash.

"I'm gonna walk down so I'll probably be a while."

"You feeling up to it?" the driver asked.

"Yeah, I haven't done anything since the shootout. I'm getting rambunctious."

Dave walked out and took a deep breath. He walked a few steps and made it to the stairway and looked down. He could hear the ocean and smell the salt air. He took his first step and could feel the stretch on his stitches and perforations. He took another and the pain seemed to ease slightly.

"Probably have to stretch," he thought.

With a death grip on the handrail, he methodically took each step sideways and rested.

Richie's head popped out from above.

"You sure you're alright?"

"Once I get going I'll be fine."

CHAPTER 40

DELAWARE VALLEY SEARCH PLAN

Greenlee Police Dispatch Console

"All departments: be on the look for four men wanted for murder, armed robbery and evading law enforcement. Four males, description to follow. Last seen driving a white minivan with Wisconsin license plate 16G-678. Subjects have been traveling east from Los Angeles / San Diego region. Possibly headed to the New York – Philadelphia - Delaware area. All men are considered armed and extremely dangerous. Description as follows:

Male #1 white male 6' brown hair 185 lbs –

Male #2 white male 6"5 approx 180 lbs, possibly early twenties, blond hair – athletic, left handed

Male #3 brown male possibly Hispanic or of Middle Eastern descent NOI.

Male #4 white male mid thirties, , 5'9" bodybuilder, possibly wounded in torso by gunshots

If located please call your local FBI headquarters or Agent

Anthony Donovan

Tom Howard pulled the print out off of the printer.

Leoni walked in with his steno pad.

"Tom, can you run these tags for me? Here's the info and the case number to reference."

"Sure thing," Howard said taking the information.

"Also, we just got a teletype about that bank robbery crew from out west. The just put out a Delaware Valley Search Plan. They think they might be in the area now."

Leoni closed his note pad and carefully placed his pen in his shirt pocket ensuring he did not get ink on his clothing.

"I'll put it on my daily report. Chances are slim that they'd come here."

"It's just that ..."

Leoni walked out of the room ignoring the dispatcher.

Victoria turned and looked at Tom.

"He's got bigger problems to worry about."

"His gun?"

Victoria rolled her chair closer.

"It seems he swore he didn't take his gun with him to the Circus Tavern but the custodian there found it under a table by the dance floor."

"Hmmm. That's not good."

"A little bird told me he's about to get booted out of the dick bureau," Victoria whispered.

Tom sat back in his chair and looked at the teletype. He pressed the microphone transmit button.

"Sarge, can you give me a call when you get a minute?"

"10-4," was Morrow's reply.

Victoria looked over at Tom.

"Anything interesting?"

Tom passed the print out to her.

"Probably not but I just want to pass this along… just in case."

The phone rang seconds later and Howard answered.

"I just wanted to pass on the info about the robbery crew that might be in our area- one guy is a blonde haired guy that is six foot five."

"OK. You sound like you have something else to tell me."

"I saw a guy that size getting coffee on my way to work. He was big; young but very tall. He looked like a human giraffe."

"What time?"

"About seven o'clock at the Shop All Night Mart."

"Did you notice a car?"

"No. I saw him inside the store."

"We'll set up there tomorrow at the same time to see if he comes back. Don't say anything on the air but I'll text everyone and let them know," Morrow told him.

"Want me to make copies of the teletype so you can pass them on."

"Sounds good."

"I just didn't want to let it go without saying something to someone."

"Sure. Thanks. He shouldn't be too hard to find if he is that tall."

"Probably not."

Sergeant Morrow rode by the Shop All Night Mart and breezed in the front door. Police work. Real police work. Possibly. Not probably.

"At least an exercise to brush up on my skills," he thought. If the robbery crew was in Greenlee, he wanted to be the one who found them.

"Was anyone here working at 7:00 A.M. this morning?"

"I was," a fiftyish looking woman said. Morrow motioned for her to meet him in the office. Inside he took out his note book.

"Do you remember a tall young man in here this morning?"

"Yeah, he was big. Nice looking kid though."

"Do you remember what he bought?"

"Ground coffee, half and half, milk, toilet paper and a cherry cheese danish. A big one. I remember thinking he must have just arrived in town."

"Do you remember anything else about him? Tattoos, accent, scars, anything?"

"No, nothing stands out, just his height."

"Can I look at the tape?"

"Sure, give me a few minutes."

Morrow began texting the men and women on the shift, Captain Fertid and Chief Wilson:

Note all: Familiarize yourselves with the "Skeleton Crew" bank robbery crew. Tom Howard saw a young man about six foot five at the Shop All Night Mart this morning. I'm here now. Manager is pulling the tape. Just in case these guys are in town. Don't get caught flat footed.

Morrow slid his phone into his front pants pocket. The manager could hear his phone buzzing in his pants as she worked on the video system.

He pulled it out.

"7 New Text Messages"

1. From Bob Connolly: Saw them on the news. Will keep an eye out.

2. From O'Malley: Tall guy, brown guy, muscle guy and average white guy. Armed and dangerous. Got it. Any other info?

3. From Ken Bogard: Skeleton Crew here?!!! OMG!

GTFO!!!

4. Officer Gary Geeman: Will BOLO. Bad asses - be careful!

5. Big John: What the fuck would the Skeleton Crew be doing in a piss ant town like Greenlee?

6. Captain Fertid: Sending Detective Fritz down to meet you.

7. Chief Wilson: O.K. Keep me posted. Fertid will contact you.

Another buzz emanated from his phone:

"1 New text message"

From Tom Howard: He might have had a Sea Chest condos key ring in his hand when he paid for his things.

The manager waved Morrow over.

"Here it is paying for his stuff. He's a big one!

The manager watched as the clerk tallied up his items.

"Almond milk," she said. "Last item was Almond milk."

"What is it?"

"People who have trouble digesting regular milk drink it."

"I had no idea almonds had nipples."

"No. I don't think that's how it works. But it's not bad."

"So this guy or someone he is with can't drink milk?"

"Or ice cream or anything else with any dairy products

in it; unless they just like the taste of almond milk. Doubtful though."

Morrow took a few snap shots from the monitor with his cell phone. Detective Fritz walked in.

"Here he is," Morrow told Fritz without a hint of animosity.

Fritz looked at the frozen image on the monitor.

"Let's take a snapshot and send it to the FBI. It would be pretty cool if it was one of those guys, huh?"

"Not likely, but I'd like to be certain," Morrow agreed.

CHAPTER 41

THE BIG TIP

Agent Anthony Donovan walked into Edwin Brimley's office and sat down without being offered a seat. A week of flying and interviewing people was taking its toll on him. There were multiple witnesses to the murder of the bank guard and the subsequent shooting of the robber who shot the guard. Many of the witnesses were not the type of people who handled such an event well. Going over the minute details on the triple shooting was tedious and time consuming.

Brimley turned to a new page on his yellow legal pad and took out a pen. Donovan waited for him to complain about the amount of time he spent on the interviews.

"You look like hell," Brimley told him.

"I've been travelling a lot and not getting a lot of sleep."

"I've been working on a pretty shitty case myself. But first what did you find out?"

"I followed up on that tip we got about the baseball player

who fit the description of one of the bank robbers. I spoke to his mother. She says her son is in the Marines and she keeps in touch with him on Face Book. She has a picture of him on the mantle in his dress blues. Nice looking kid, good student, smart and a talented baseball player. She is as proud as can be."

"So that's a dead end?" Brimley asked.

"Actually no. I went to the recruiter's office just to verify he was in the Marines..."

"Alright...?" Brimley said scribbling on his pad.

"...and they said he failed the physical. He is lactose intolerant. He tried to get in the Navy, Army, Air Force and Coast Guard afterward. No can do... because of his problem with dairy."

"But she thinks he is in."

"Did you tell her?"

"No."

Brimley nodded in approval.

"I didn't want her to tip him off when he does call or write. I'm afraid it would rock her world. You should see her. She is old school; prim and proper, cookies and tea kind of gal. She's a sweet old thing actually."

"O.K. It's your case. You handle the way you see fit."

"Then I interviewed the probation officer that shot at them. He's been armed about twenty two years. Never fired a shot except for the range. He shoots and kills one of them, wounds another. Someone takes a shot at him and misses."

"I thought these were bad ass tactical guys."

"Me too," Donovan admitted.

"That seems strange. Maybe it just was his lucky day," Brimley mused.

"Anyway I interviewed everybody at the bank that day. A few remember the tall kid coming in and casing the place. All three think he is this young kid, Richard Armstrong. I showed them the picture of him and no one could positively ID him but everyone is guessing it was him. Then as I am finishing up there I get a call from the home office that there was a shootout where a highway patrolman was shot, and an old Native American guy was kidnapped for a short while. He wasn't helpful. Says he's too old to remember anything. He did say they gave him a hundred dollar bill for the gas and drinks they took."

"Did you take it," Brimley asked.

I did. He didn't have a problem with it either."

"Surprising."

Donovan nodded.

"I interviewed the trooper in the hospital and he confirms one of them is hurt. He seemed more upset that they shot up his car than he was about catching a ricochet in the hip."

Brimley sat back in his chair.

"These guys sound like they're pretty heavy handed."

"Wait until you hear this. Right after the highway

patrolman stopped these guys, he let them go. He didn't know they were wanted until afterward. He starts looking for the minivan they were in and they pull into the rear of a diner, get out with a video camera and tell everyone in the diner they are shooting a reality T.V. show."

"Ballsy," Brimley agreed.

"They tell them they are on a cross country race for a show called Race for Love. They buy two vehicles, tape the sales negotiation and pay these two guys with cash. They even had them sign release forms so they can use the footage on T.V. this fall."

"Pretty slick. So no one reports their cars stolen."

"The highway patrolman passes two of them in a different vehicle and he recognizes the driver. Then of course, all hell breaks loose."

"It would be nice to get that footage, just for shits and giggles if nothing else," Brimley told him, smiling.

"The next night I get a teletype from a police department that a clerk at a pharmacy remembers a tall kid coming in and buying all kinds of stuff for his friend who supposedly stepped on a nail. Gauze, peroxide, needle and thread and this is interesting; almond milk.

Brimley's eyes widened.

"Almond milk. My wife drinks almond milk. She'd shit her pants if she drank the real stuff. So that fits in with this Armstrong fellow. Sounds like you are on the trail."

"While I was in town I checked with the local gyms,

shooting ranges, gun shops and other pharmacies, hospitals and clinics. I don't think they stayed in town very long."

Brimley's phone rang startling both men.

"Yes. He's right here."

Brimley handed the phone to Donovan.

"Donovan… sure. Can you e-mail it to me? I'd be happy to. I appreciate your efforts. One question; do you know what he bought?

Donovan wrote on a pad and gave his boss a hopeful look.

"I see. I'll give you a call as soon as I see it. I'll send you a picture of a young man I suspect is one of them. I'll call you back at this number.""

"Well? "

"A Detective from Greenlee, New Jersey has a video of a tall kid at a store in their town. He was buying coffee and creamer and danish and…"

"Almond milk?" Brimley hoped out loud.

Donovan nodded.

"When?"

"This morning." Donovan's voice deepened as he smiled.

"Nice work. Call the local office and see if they can lend a hand. Then grab the next flight. When you get a tip like this you have to jump right on it."

Donovan nodded wearily.

"Now get down there and grab these guys."

"On the way," Donovan said as he pulled himself out of the chair.   "You've done some nice work on this case. Getting the word out to the public was a good move."

CHAPTER 42

ON THE HEELS OF THE SKELETON CREW

Greenlee, N.J.

Richie waded through the surf and dodged a child on a Styrofoam surfboard. As he made his way through the children and parents and teenagers he noticed how the younger men seemed to be a little more rambunctious than the rest. He noticed the middle aged men doing their best to hold in their stomachs and pushing their chests out. The elderly men mostly stood there admiring everyone else with no regard for their lost physique; pot bellies and fluffy white fur protruding from their chests and shoulders. A few had scars from surgeries, some had tattoos. As he watched the women, he noticed the older women seemed so carefree in their floral one pieces or variations of it. Some had short skirts attached and others had huge sunglasses and floppy seventies style hats to protect them from the sun. The women in their twenties to their forties flaunted what they had, most of them. A few softies were covered up, not ready to show the world what had happened to their curves. Then he saw her; a statuesque brunette walking slowly down the beach. Big dark sunglasses, solemn look on her face and a long lean body. She was in a one piece medium blue bathing suit with a small cord ankle bracelet.

As she walked toward him he wondered what her eyes were looking at. He noticed her veer slightly his way, ever so slightly. Or was it just wishful thinking? Richie looked at her. He couldn't help but look at her. After so many days on the road, being pursued and hiding out, Richie suddenly felt alive again, buoyed by the roar of the surf, the pleasant stinging of the salt air and sun tan lotion, the hot sun on his shoulders and the warm breeze up his shorts.

"Uh hi," the beautiful woman said to him as he stood motionless.

"Hello yourself," he said.

"What the fuck is wrong with you," he thought as the woman tilted her head.

"Do you know where, like, any good parties are tonight?" She sang the word "parties" for emphasis.

"I don't. I'm not from around here."

"Wull, Ya'ah," she giggled.

"Like, no one is from around here. We're at the Jersey shore."

"I can't argue with that," he said turning slightly away from the water.

Over her shoulder he could see their condo just across the street. The main road was littered with police cars and what appeared to be a S.W.A.T. team was huddled in the parking garage while patrol officers and special police officers ushered pedestrians away. A crowd from the beach was gathering. Richie's heart sank knowing whomever was still inside their condos were probably done for.

Inside, Mooj heard the police moving in downstairs. The apartment below once occupied by Dave and Richie had been compromised. The driver packed all of the money into a black duffel bag. Looking out the window toward the street he could see at least six police cars of varying types. His heart raced. He could feel men rushing up the wooden stairs at the side of the condominium complex. He put all of the weapons under the bed in the rear bedroom with the ammunition and trench coats. Mooj looked out the front window overlooking the wooden walkway between the rows of condos. He could see a uniformed police officer knocking on the door across the way. He strained to listen.

"We're evacuating the building. Everyone must leave. This is an emergency."

Mooj ducked down.

"Go to the door! Cops are telling everyone to evacuate."

The driver stood by the door and waited for the knock. He opened the door.

"We're evacuating the building. This is an emergency," the officer said in a slightly hushed but forceful tone.

"Let me grab my keys. Can I help?"

"No thank you sir, we're good. Please hurry!"

Dave sprinted back to the bedroom. Mooj was looking out the back window.

"I'll leave the truck for you at Ninth street. You know where to meet us."

Mooj nodded, obviously worried.

"I have your money. Everything else is tucked under the bed. Best not get caught in here."

"Good luck," Mooj told him.

The driver threw the beach bag over his shoulder and headed out. Mooj watched him walk out the door with the money; *all* of the money. He knew he could trust the driver. There had been many opportunities to run off with the money if he was so inclined. They all had an opportunity at one time or another. They had never been in a scrape like this. Not since the shootout when Carlos was killed.

"Getting away clean, even without the money would be a victory," Mooj thought. He paced back and forth. He could see more police cars pulling up. He knew his brownness would be a problem.

"Mooj!"

It was the driver. Get out here quick. Mooj ran to the door.

"Give these people a hand please."

The driver winked at him.

Mooj looked out of the door and the Pakistani family was evacuating and trying to get their ancient grandmother out in a timely fashion. The father had his two young daughters in his arms, the mother a baby and her mother by the hand. He took the grandmother by the hand and swooped her up and seemed to blend in with the family. No one would notice he did not bear the same features or body type as the Pakistani family. As far as anyone was concerned, he was brown like the rest of them. Brown with straight hair. Problem solved.

Dave slipped through the people walking briskly down the steps. Mooj carried the elderly woman down the steps and gently put her down.

"Dan kyew, dan kyew," the father said slightly bowing.

"Perhaps we should move away in case it is a fire or a gas leak," Mooj suggested.

He surveyed the area. A large crowd had gathered on the beach across the street from the condo. In the distance he could see Richie talking to a woman by the water's edge.

Behind him he could hear police radios, and police talking amongst themselves and to the crowd that had gathered. As he looked up at the building he could see a helmeted S.W.A.T. officer sticking his head out of the window of what *was* Dave and Richie's condo. He wondered what clues were left behind. Money? Phones? Maps? As he stood on the beach surrounded by his newly adopted Pakistani family, he knew he had to get out quickly.

"Hey! Do you want to take a walk," Richie said to the beautiful young woman in front of him.

"Wuhl, SURE," she said eagerly.

He led her in the direction she was walking and hoped

she wouldn't see the commotion behind her.

"So like, how old are you?"

"Nineteen," Richie admitted.

"Wow. How old do you think I am," she teased.

"Well, when I first saw you I thought you were about twenty five, but now I'm not so sure."

"Uh, ye'ah, I get that alot, like *ALL* the time."

"So how old are you?"

Her head bobbed from side to side ever so slightly. She stopped. Her left leg slid back as if to steady herself.

"I'll be eighteen, soon."

"So you are seventeen now?"

She paused.

"Uh…,"

"Sixteen?"

"Well in a about two-"

"Fifteen? Fifteen years old?"

Her head hung down.

"Like, wh'y is it such like a big dee'al?"

"Well it's like this, " Richie said trying to come up with a family rated version of the birds and the bees and criminal law involving sex with minors as he slowly and methodically escaped from what was sure death and or capture back at the condo.

"People assume that a young man my age is interested in one thing and that they will try to take advantage of a young girl like you. Many guys would try. It just doesn't look right to older people."

"Rachel," an older man yelled from a group of sunbathers and kite fliers.

"Oh Gawd. My dad."

"Let's go say hello," Richie told her.

"Who is your friend?"

Richie put his hand out.

"Richard."

The man shook his hand.

"Bob Allen," the man replied.

"We're having some burgers. Come join us."

An ambulance flew down the road just off the beach and everyone stopped to watch it. Richie's stomach was suddenly flooded with acid.

"Busy day for the public servants," Bob said handing Richie a burger.

"Sure is."

Bob moved in a little closer.

"Just so we are on the same page son, did Rachel tell you how old she was?"

"She was just telling me as we got here. Fifteen."

Bob let out a sigh.

"Fourteen. Fourteen years old."

Richie looked at the man.

"I don't envy you sir," Richie told him.

Dave carried both bags out the front door of the convenience store. He moved some items from one bag to another to balance them out. The weigh pulled on his wounds as the plastic bags swung back and forth. As he walked in the summer sun, he could feel his energy being sapped. He looked down the long avenue littered with ice cream shops, a surf supply store and restaurants. All of the down time had robbed him of his endurance. Surely one of the guys would come looking for him he hoped. As he took each step he could feel the fatigue and now the soreness in his stomach increased. His steps got smaller and smaller, his pace slowed.

The heat seemed to be cooking him as he stood on the sidewalk. He pushed on but as he moved he could tell he wouldn't make it much further. A small, run down car pulled up next to him and the passenger window came down.

"Hey hernia guy! You o.k.?"

"Crystal," he said squinting into the car.

"Actually it's Ann. You need a ride?"

"Yes," he said as he stood on the sidewalk almost too weak to move. He dropped his bags.

The stripper got out of her car and opened the passenger door.

"Get in," she said taking him by the arms. Dave sat in the front seat and Ann put his groceries in the back and got back in the car.

"You don't look so good," she told him.

"I think I bit off more than I can chew."

"I'll take you home," she offered.

"No! My roommates are ... busy... busy with their girlfriends. Can I buy you lunch?"

"You feel up to it?"

"Sure. Pick somewhere."

Ann drove a few blocks down and stopped at McHugh's pizzeria and parked out front. Inside they took a window seat overlooking the main drag.

As they ate Dave could feel the air-conditioning bringing him back to life. He seemed to get stronger the cooler he got.

"I'm really sorry about last night. I felt bad afterwards."

"No, it was all my fault. I shouldn't have gone out in the first place. I've just been so bored being laid up."

"So you guys are on vacation together," she asked.

"It's a working vacation."

"What kind of work do you do? You *know* what kind of work I do."

"Banking. We upgrade security systems. We're waiting for the new hardware to get here. We'll probably have a few days to play before we get to work."

As he spoke two Atlantic City police cars sped by.

"Strange," she said.

Dave took another bite of his pizza.

"The cops aren't looking for you, are they," he joked, worried about the apartment and his team.

"Well… not for anything that would require all of this. I might have some unpaid parking tickets. You're not going to turn me in are you?"

"No. But I do get excited around dangerous women."

She laughed and held his hand.

"You look so different than you did last night. You look like the girl next door."

"Thanks, I think."

Another Atlantic City police car sped by with its lights on.

Dave's heart sank as he saw a blacked out SUV speed by a few seconds later. He wished he had his phone, his car or one of the guys with him. In his weakened condition he wasn't sure how far he could get.

As they finished their drinks, Dave saw a familiar face walking by. He knocked on the glass and Richie looked in. Dave waved him in. Richie looked scared and unsure of himself.

As he walked in he looked at Ann.

"Crystal?"

"Ann."

"Good to see you again," he said, about to burst.

"Looks like something going on down the other end of the Avenue," Dave told him.

"Yeah, on Thirteenth street," Richie told him confirming what Dave had already suspected.

"Dave, I think we have to get going. The parts are in. We have to get them before FEDEX closes."

Ann looked at Dave.

"You have to go?"

"For a while. Can I call you?"

"Sure. You know where to find me."

She scribbled her phone number on a napkin.

"Let me give you a ride."

"My truck is just around the corner. But thanks anyway," Richie said hurriedly.

Dave shrugged his shoulders and left two twenties on the table.

"Take care of the tab for me?"

As Dave got up so did Richie and Ann. Ann gave Dave a hug until he winced in pain.

"Oh my God I forgot, I am so sorry!"

Dave smiled despite the pain.

"I'll call you soon."

As the two men left hurriedly Ann sat back down and snatched the pizza crust from Dave's plate. She munched on it and watched the men disappear around the corner.

A moment later two police officers appeared at the back door of the restaurant. Another car pulled up out front with four officers in full SWAT gear and approached the pizza parlor cautiously. As they entered the red haired pizza cook behind the counter pointed to Ann. The men approached the table. Anthony Donovan walked in the front door and approached her as the SWAT officers stepped back watching the surrounding area.

"Special Agent Donovan," he said flashing his identification and badge at the young woman.

"I need to ask you some questions."

43

Shoot Out!

Absecon N.J.

Doug O'Malley took a deep breath. He enjoyed not being constricted by his body armor. His brown canvas work pants and work boots felt light compared to his uniform. He enjoyed not having everyone staring at him as he made his way up and down the aisles.

In the plumbing department with his girlfriend, he watched as she scoped out the different types of sinks and counter tops. As April ran her hand along the smoothly finished granite, she imaged what they might look like in her home. Doug watched as the contractors made their way down the aisle, each one taking a quick glance at his girlfriend. He didn't mind. April was a beautiful girl with a great figure and sweet personality. She didn't seem to notice that most men are pigs. If she did, she didn't let on.

"Wouldn't this look nice," she asked.

"Sure," he answered.

"A sturdy surface to make sandwiches," he thought.

He was happy to help her with her new kitchen. It was time to blow a day off. He found himself wondering why he didn't do it more often. He loved police work and the daily routine of having no routine. He loved the vast variety of calls for service. Once he was off, he discovered he loved doing other things too, maybe not as much a police work, but he did like working with tools and home improvement projects despite uneven results.

He felt his pocket buzz. Pulling out his phone he saw he had a text message:

From Ken Bogard:

"Big doin's today. FBI is in town looking for the bank robbery crew. Skeleton Crew."

"Damn," he said under his breath.

"What's wrong," April asked.

"It looks like the shit is hitting the fan at work."

"Do you have to go?"

"Nah, the FBI is there. I'm sure they'll be o.k. without me."

O'Malley texted a message back to Bogard:

"Picking out counter tops."

O'Malley let out a deep breath and tried to concentrate on his task at hand.

"Chief ordered sub trays, gonna be a big operation no doubt," was the next text message he received from Bogard.

He shook his head and smiled.

Doug took the sketch he made of April's existing countertop and tallied up the measurements. He began to compute the cost of the particular stone countertop April preferred as a sturdy sandwich making area.

"Ping!" Doug's phone chimed.

"Raid at Sea Chest! Big crowds, looks like the siege at

Waco!"

Bogard was surely breaking his balls. He stood listening to April as she analyzed the difference of having one highly polished rock counter as opposed to another slightly darker highly polished stone counter.

"Who the fuck cares," he thought, nodding in false concern.

"This will look great with the roasted chestnut paint trim on the cabinets. Did I show you the roasted chestnut trim paint for the cabinets?"

Doug nodded, his mind wandering now.

"Oh look at these knobs on the drawers here. These would look great. I wonder if you can buy the knobs separately. Let's stop by the paint department. I'd like to get a swatch of the roasted chestnut to hold up with these knobs and see if they really go together. What do you think?"

Doug looked at her. His eyes were looking but not seeing. He was somewhere else. April hated when he got like this.

"You want to be in on the action. Whatever is going on at work," she told him.

"Does it show that much?"

She looked at him, her face oozing with sarcasm.

"I'm sure it'll be over by the time we leave the parking lot if it isn't over all ready. "

"You sure?"

"Yes," he said hoping it was true.

"Which do you like best? Or do you want to keep looking," he asked her trying to get back on track.

"Which do you like?"

Doug threw his keys on each of the counters that were in the final running. The second one had a nice solid sound when his keys were tossed.

"This one. I like the way it sounds."

April turned slowly and flashed her best "Are you friggin' kidding me," look.

Standing in the checkout line Doug watched another would be craftsman wearing a well worn Montreal Expos baseball hat. The man was struggling with two large pieces of plywood. Doug grabbed an end and helped him stand the plywood sideways on the metal cart. April placed her items on the belt by the cashier and reached into her purse and pulled out her cash. Doug scanned the area as he always did when the cash was out. Nothing. A few perplexed people walking around a giant store looking for something.

"Ping," his pocket erupted.

Text message from Bogard –

"Skeleton Crew was here. Gone. Just missed them."

Doug shook his head, annoyed. April looked at him knowingly.

"Well?"

"The Skeleton Crew, the bank robbers that have been on the news, they were in Greenlee and just made a quick getaway. They just missed them."

"If you were there they wouldn't have gotten away," April told him trying to hide the fact that she didn't want him involved in any of this business of arresting bank robbers.

As Doug and April walked into the parking lot Doug's phone rang.

"Ken! What the hell is going on there?"

"You picked a hell of a day to take off. Those fuckers were here. We only missed them by a few minutes, maybe a half hour."

"I wish I could have been there. I'm helping April with her new kitchen, looking at counter tops."

Doug looked up and saw the six foot five Rich Armstrong walking in between a minivan and a pickup truck.

Doug lowered his voice.

"Ken, THEY'RE HERE, at the Builder's Paradise. In the parking lot. I'll try to tail them. Notify Absecon!"

Doug took his girlfriend by the arm.

"They're here!"

"Who?"

"The Skeleton Crew. Go inside, the police are on the way. Run!"

"But, but …"

Doug pushed her in the direction of the door and she ran.

Richie walked briskly through the parking lot. Doug could tell he was looking for something or someone. Richie's head swayed back and forth. Doug touched the outside of his right front pants pocket. He felt it. His seven shot .380 semi automatic pistol. He felt better as he tailed Armstrong through the lot. Suddenly Armstrong spun and locked eyes with him in a reflection from a minivan window. He turned and Doug approached him.

"Excuse me? Do you have any jumper cables?"

"No, sorry," Richie said eyeing him up and down.

"I'm in a rush."

"Oh, we have a baby inside the truck."

"Sorry man," Armstrong said trotting away. Doug followed him when a shot rang out, whizzing past Armstrong and striking a side view mirror next to O'Malley.

O'Malley ducked and pulled out his pistol; his "lady gun" as Big John called it. He raised it and scanned the area. Another pop was heard. A "thunk" sounded as the same vehicle was hit by a second bullet.

Richie took off in a full run disappearing in the midst of several parked trucks. Slowly, O'Malley moved forward trying to find out where the shots came from. It was oddly quiet. No radio to yell into, no one pointing, running or waving their arms.

O'Malley crept through the next row of cars and trucks keeping low. Traffic flew by on the highway just outside of the parking lot. Out of the corner of his eye he saw the Montreal Expos baseball hat appear and then the man wearing it, pushing the cart with the plywood. Then his wife also appeared from behind a large SUV.

He tried to wave them away without saying anything. The man looked straight ahead as did his wife. Doug waved at them again but they kept looking forward, then at each other. The man ran to his wife, grabbed her and they both disappeared behind a truck. Suddenly from behind the plywood on the cart a heavily muscled man popped up and fired another shot. Doug raised his pistol to fire but traffic flew by behind the man.

The man ran and O'Malley chased him. A large red extended cab pickup truck rolled down the parking lot. Doug looked up at the driver who locked in on the gun in Doug's hand. Doug waved him away. The driver put the large truck in reverse and backed quickly down the aisle, around the corner and then floored the massive truck out of the parking lot.

Doug could see the reflection of black military style boots under a parked car in a puddle. He gave chase. As he approached the man from behind, he could see a black semi-automatic handgun in the man's hand.

"Freeze," Doug commanded.

The man turned and fired another shot at Doug who raised his pistol but noticed the man with the Montreal Expos hat squatting on the ground shielding his wife behind his target.

"Four shots," Doug thought. No sirens, flashing lights, radio chatter indicating back up was on the way. Dodging bullets but unable to squeeze off one of his own, O'Malley slowly pursued the gunman throughout the parking lot. His only strategy was to keep them in the parking lot until back up arrived. He wondered if Bogard had heard him say they were there. He wondered if Bogard had relayed the message to the dispatcher or if he just broadcasted the information himself on the county radio band.

As the gunman fired another round, O'Malley ducked behind an old truck. The bullet whizzed by. O'Malley popped his head around the corner to see a large green SUV pull up in the next aisle, the driver waving to the gunman to come his way. As the muscular gunman ran toward the green SUV, it's driver pointed a pistol at Doug.

Frustrated with what seemed to be a gunfight that no one else could see or hear, Doug fired at the driver and charged the vehicle.

Taking a half dozen steps, he could see the driver stick his head up and Doug took another shot. He charged the vehicle in a full run and lept onto the running board reached inside and fired one more round into the driver who was now obviously dead. The passenger door flew open and the muscular gunman raised his gun at Doug but Doug had the drop on him and fired first hitting the man in the chest, twice.

"Probably the bastard that was shooting at me," Doug thought.

Doug scanned the interior of the truck which was empty. The man in the Montreal baseball hat popped his head up but still had his arms over his wife's head.

"Are you a cop?"

"Yes. Do me a favor. When the police get here, just put your hands straight up in the air until things settle down."

Doug could hear sirens approaching from the east. Another police car pulled into the lot at the opposite end. Doug slipped his gun back in his pocket and pulled out his badge and held it up high. The police car came to a skidding stop the officer jumped out with his gun drawn.

"I'm a police officer! I'm the one that made the report."

"I recognize you," the Absecon Officer said.

The uniformed police officer approached the SUV, weapon held close to his body when he saw the two dead men. One in the driver's seat, the other half in the passenger seat, his lower half still dangling outside. His gun lay on the parking lot.

"Two dead, the tall male is on foot in the area," O'Malley told the uniformed officer.

"These two are witnesses," he said gesturing to the man in the Montreal Expos hat and his wife.

They both slowly got up off of the ground.

The man's wife looked at Doug.

"They were trying to kill you," she said.

"Yes ma'am. But I wasn't having it today".

As the blacked out SUV's started gathering in the parking lot agent Anthony Donovan approached Doug.

"You o.k.?"

"Yep. Let me go tell my girlfriend I'm alright but the tall kid with the blonde hair got away, on foot."

A grizzled bearded man wearing painter's pants and a denim shirt approached the officers.

"Someone stole my truck."

"What did it look like?"

"Can't miss it. Bright red extended cab pickup truck. It sits high."

"I waved him off while I was chasing the muscleman here," O'Malley confessed. Doug made his way to the front of the store where April was waiting. He waited for her to burst into tears when she saw him.

"Well?"

"I got two of them."

"What the fuck," she said.

Doug was taken aback.

"You only get two out of four of them?"

"I only had my pea shooter with me or I'd have had all four," he told her, smiling.

April looked out onto the parking lot which was now jam packed with marked and unmarked police cars and several officers.

"Do we really need all of these flashing lights? It's a parking lot for God's sake."

Doug really didn't know what had gotten into April but he liked it.

CHAPTER 44

SPIRITED AWAY

Absecon, N.J.

Mooj drove the red extended cab pickup down a cul de sac and parked it. Richie climbed out of the bed of the truck.

"That was close."

"I haven't heard from Dave or the driver," Mooj said.

"What did we come away with?"

Mooj reached in and pulled out four large nylon duffel bags.

"All of it," Mooj told him.

"We can't drive around in this thing," he said gesturing to the mammoth pickup truck.

"I know who I can call," Richie told him. He reached in his pocket and pulled out Carlos' phone.

He scrolled to the contacts list of which there was only one, he dialed.

"Yes?" the voice on the other end answered.

"I don't know who you are but I used to work with Carlos"

"You did, huh?"

"Not anymore obviously. We're in a bind. Can you help us?"

"Where's Daryl?"

"Who?"

"Your team leader."

"We only knew him by his nickname. Driver."

"Daryl River. D. River…driver."

Richie shook his head at the simplicity.

"We were at our emergency evacuation spot and something went wrong. There was a shoot out and we have no idea where the other two are or if they are alright."

"Where are you guys?"

"Absecon, New Jersey."

"Is that near Atlantic City?"

"About twenty minutes out."

"What's near you?"

"Two bars, the Hi Point and The Black Cat, near the Sunoco station."

"I'll have a young black man meet you at the Hi Point."

"When you see him, tell him to pull up his pants, then he'll know you're with us."

"Got it. Thanks."

"One more thing, from now on, you can call me anytime day or night but only on the half hour. Any other time and I'll assume someone else has the phone and I won't answer from that number again. Same for you. If you get a call from this number and it isn't on the half hour, assume the phone has been compromised."

Mooj and Richie grabbed their duffels and hastily made their way to the Hi Point Lounge. As they walked in they made their way to the bar which was almost filled. They watched the crowd and pretended to watch the ball game on the large television there.

A tidy looking black man walked in, smartly dressed in khaki pants, golf shirt which revealed a trim physique and an oversized, overly shiny watch.

"I'm guessing that is not our man," Mooj said. Richie nodded in agreement. He sat down at the bar and was greeted warmly by the bartender.

As the front door opened another African American walked in. He was dressed in baggy pants barely hanging onto the equator of his buttocks. A large baggy sweatshirt and decades old bomber jacket could be hiding several weapons. His hairdo could be described as erratic. The man had an angry look on his face. He seemed to be daring anyone to take a look at him for more than fraction of a second.

"That's gotta be our man," Richie whispered glancing over

his beer. Mooj nodded and watched as the angry looking man circled around the bar and headed their way. As the man approached, Mooj spoke softly.

"Pull up your fucking pants."

"Say WHAT," the angry man retorted leaning into Mooj. Richie put his foot up against the duffel bags that were sitting on the floor by their bar stools.

"Yo! Chief," Richie said putting his hand on the man's chest. Other patrons began to stand up.

"I'll beat both your asses right here!" the angry man told them.

"Gentlemen," the preppy looking black man appeared, seemingly out of nowhere.

"We have a mutual friend," he said.

"That remark was meant for me, as a joke. They didn't mean anything by it."

The angry man still seemed angry but dropped his hands off of both men.

"Let me buy you a beer. We're not looking for trouble," Mooj told him.

Before the man could answer Mooj and Richie picked up their bags and Mooj put two twenty dollars bills on the bar.

"Cool?"

"Cool."

"We have a train to catch," Richie told the neatly dressed

black man.

"Come on, let's go."

"I'll be glad when this day is over," Mooj said.

"I'm thinking it is over for Dave and the Driver."

CHAPTER 45

WINTER BALL

San Juan, Puerto Rico

Richie grabbed his bags and stood up as soon as the bus stopped in the parking lot. As the others gathered their bags he stepped out and looked at the lush green grass and felt the heat hit him despite the early hour.

He felt the butterflies in his stomach. He hadn't been to tryouts for quite a while. In high school he was a shoe in to make the team. His strong arm and competitive nature assured him a spot as a starting pitcher; but now he had to prove himself all over again.

"Harvey Haslett," he heard a voice behind him yell. He didn't react at first but then realized that was the alias he was using.

"Yes sir," he barked trying to make up for lost time.

"Go warm up."

Richie nodded and pulled his glove out of his bag and

trotted up to the plate where a catcher was fastening his shin guards.

"Give it all you've got," the catcher said as Richie adjusted his cap and headed for the mound.

Richie looked at the men standing by the dugout. Although he had arrived two days late for tryouts there were still a few scouts around. They were watching him but he could see they were making comments back and forth among themselves.

After some stretching he began throwing some soft pitches and began steadily increasing their speed.

"Looks like he's got a little zip," one of the scouts said.

As Richie started throwing harder and harder, he noticed a muscular player approach the plate from the right side. The catcher trotted up from the plate.

"Throw whatever you want. They're just looking to see if he can make contact with your pitches. They're looking for speed and movement. Don't get rattled if he knocks you around. Each pitch you throw is its own. There are no strikeouts, just contact or no contact."

Richie nodded as the catcher went back.

The first pitch he threw was a looping curve ball. He could see the batters eyes following it as he swung. Almost eight feet off the ground the ball seemed to stop at the plate and drop to the side.

The familiar popping sound of the ball in the catcher's mitt delighted him as well as the scouts. He could see the catcher smiling as he threw the ball back at him.

Pitch number two was a high fast ball right down the middle of the plate. The batter swung, got a piece of it and sent the ball screaming into the group of five scouts causing them to scatter. One of the men hit the dirt amid some laughter. As the batter dug in Richie caught his breath.

"That was close," he thought as he caught a new ball.

The next three pitches were fastballs. The first one was a full swing and a miss. The second was hit but bounced off of home plate and dribbled toward the mound. The third was fouled off and sailed over the group of scouts.

"Is this guy trying to hurt us?"

Richie caught a new ball and leaned forward and peered in at the catcher as though he was giving signs. He wasn't. Richie shook off the blank stare from the catcher who then caught on to what Richie was doing. He shook off another nonexistent sign then nodded with a sneer. He stood straight and took a deep breath as he had done prior to the last fastball he threw. The he wound up and threw. The ball started in high again.

"Curve ball," the batter thought in a fraction of a second and swung. A second later the ball dropped into the catcher's mitt. The man with the radar gun smothered a smile when he read "57" on the screen of the radar gun. The scouts allowed themselves to look at each other. Even the batter smiled. Richie was having his way with him. As the scouts were writing in their notebooks, Richie began to feel that he was getting into the groove.

CHAPTER 46

LEONI & FROST REGROUP

Officer Leoni parked his patrol car in the parking lot of the bowling alley on the main road through Greenlee pretending to monitor traffic. He sipped his coffee and tried to reacquaint himself with the numerous knobs and switches in the car. Shot gun release, trunk, roof lights, flashers, alley lights, take down lights, air horn, two radios and a charger for his portable radio not to mention video equipment. He pecked away at the buttons and realized it was all coming back to him. A familiar station wagon pulled up alongside him.

"How are you doing young man?"

"Been better," he said dejectedly "but I'm not licked yet."

"No you aren't, and here's why. I just talked to the City Manager and he's agreed that the department is top heavy with rank. We're cancelling the sergeant's test and trimming down by attrition. How long are you barred from competing for promotion?

"One year," Leoni said hopefully.

"One year. It looks like you're in patrol for right now but at least no one will be promoted ahead of you."

Leoni shook his head in disbelief and smiled.

"You are something else."

"I told you before; if you're in trouble, change the rules. Only suckers play by the rules."

Frost patted him on the arm.

"Stick with me kid. Oh, who is the guy you think took your gun?"

"Bob Connolly."

"Well, fuck him. He doesn't know it but I think it's time to put the pressure on him. I'll figure out something."

"Thanks, Mr. Frost, I appreciate your support."

"Don't mention it, you, me and a few others will be running this town soon."

"Oh, here are some more tapes for you."

Leoni handed Councilman Frost a handful of micro-cassette tapes.

"I love listening to these. How do you get this stuff?"

"It's easy. I turn on the tape recorder, put it in my jacket and walk into a room and take my jacket off and put it on the back of a chair. I make a remark or two then walk out and leave my jacket there to record what they say about me and sometimes you too."

Frost smiled at the officer.

"Pretty slick."

"Sometimes I put the recorder in my backpack. You gotta switch it up sometimes."

"I'll go home and listen to these."

Leoni held his finger up.

"Nothing about local drug sales. So far no one seems to know."

Frost put his car in gear.

"Good to know. The gossip is pretty entertaining too."

Leoni put his patrol car in gear. The councilman pulled away slowly and Leoni reached into his shirt pocket and turned off his tape recorder.

BRIMLEY'S BIG BUST

Anthony Donovan pecked away at the keyboard putting the finishing touches on his investigation report; two dead, two still at large, and a trail that had gone very cold. He picked up the skeleton mask that was on the top of the pile of three. The spray of blood had turned to a maroonish brown. It was one of the most interesting pieces of evidence he had ever handled. He wondered if he would ever catch the man who wore the mask during a dozen or so bank robberies. Richard Armstrong was on the run, his parents had recently vacated their home, and left no forwarding.

Brimley walked up behind him and saw Donovan admiring the mask.

"That will make a nice trophy once you catch him."

"I was thinking the same thing. Maybe it would inspire me to work harder on the case."

Brimley took the mask for a moment and examined it.

"You did a nice job. You enlisted the help of the public

which was wise, did meticulous follow up work and we at least know the identity of one of the bandits still at large. So far so good."

"It would be nice to have the whole head instead of a mask," Donovan told him.

"Do you remember Agent Tizol you met in my office? The one that transferred from Newark?" Brimley asked.

"Yes. The guy from Operation Dog and Pony."

"What did you think of him?"

Donovan paused to pick his words very carefully as the agent was one of the most high profile F.B.I. agents since his string of organized crime arrests.

"To be honest, Tizol didn't really seem like he fit the mold. A little too—ah—"

"Mobbed up?"

"Yes. Not very businesslike."

"Well, he was just scooped up by the Bureau of Professional Responsibility. His arrests were propped up with some fabricated evidence and two informants who say he actually killed two people while undercover."

"They were actually two informants I used when I was assigned to Newark. I always kept in touch. Good thing."

"You seemed like you were under a little stress lately," Donovan noted.

"Do you remember the Greenlee cops that were suspected of killing a gangster's son while he was in custody?"

"Yes, I met them while I was in Greenlee. Interesting group I have to say."

Brimley lowered his voice.

"Well the dead gangster's father is one of the eight people who have petitioned for release and a new trial."

"Think he's got a score to settle?"

"Wouldn't you," Brimley asked smiling.

CHAPTER 48

FILMORE'S DINER

Jack Duffield walked into the diner to find sergeant Morrow, Big John and Connolly sitting in their corner booth. He scooted into the booth and held up an empty coffee cup, catching Sally's eye. She moved in and filled it.

"Well? What's the big news?"

Morrow raised an eyebrow smugly and adjusted his tie. He cleared his throat. Smothering a smile he leaned over the table and everyone drew near.

"Leoni was put back in patrol and pulled off the test for sergeant."

"Holy shit," Connolly said.

"Holy shit indeed," Morrow said smiling.

"How about the Internal Affairs investigation? Fritz was like a dog on a bone," Big John asked pulling his paper napkin out of his collar.

"Turns out he was bluffing the whole time. He was onto

us though. I knew Frank would never give me up. Not in a million years."

Sally scanned the room for eavesdroppers.

"You have to stop these shenanigans. They're going to catch up to you."

Morrow and Big John nodded in agreement.

"That's how we stay sharp," Connolly told her.

Ken Bogard whizzed by the diner and whipped a quick u-turn and pulled into the lot. As he sprung up the steps Big John turned to Morrow.

"He looks like he has news."

Bogard walked in and tried to force his way in the booth but Big John wouldn't budge.

"Come on John."

He shook his head dejectedly and pulled a chair from an empty table and sat.

"Sergeants test is cancelled. They want to trim down the department by attrition. No test."

No one said anything at first.

"Do you know how much I paid for those books," Connolly asked.

"About four hundred dollars."

"Yes."

Morrow stared into space for a moment.

"You know what this means? It means Leoni has a pretty powerful ally. We better be on our toes."

"I could write a book about this place" Big John said through his disillusionment.

"You can't even fill out a simple accident report," Connolly chided him.

"I'll be filling out your death certificate if you don't watch it."

Morrow looked at Bogard and shook his head in resignation. Sally wandered off to serve her customers and Jack Duffield sat back with his coffee watching the officers finish up their breakfast.

"Just a reminder guys," Duffield said.

"Do you know how many people would give their right arm to be a cop?" The remark took a moment to sink in and Sergeant Morrow was the first to chime in.

"How about if we go out and catch criminals? That's why we're here anyway …not to line our pockets with gold. We are here to serve the public."

Connolly handed Sally the check with cash.

"Keep the change."

Connolly, Morrow and Bogard filed out and Big John watched them. Duffield downed his coffee and rose from the table.

"Very inspiring speech but you're going to bed aren't you?"

"I am."

Big John's cell phone buzzed.

Text Message from Morrow:

"Chief wants to see you, me and Connolly in his office pronto!"

Big John shook his head.

"Or not."

CHAPTER 49

DISTURBING NEWS

The Chief was visibly upset when Bob Connolly walked into his office.

"Have a seat Bob," he said waving Captain Fertid in from the hallway.

Morrow walked in and Connolly shot him a look.

"This won't be good," Morrow thought.

Big John sauntered in, looking worn out and beat down from having been up all night.

"I have a date with my bed Chief. Can we make this quick?"

The Chief didn't react to the remark which told the men something serious was happening.

"Is this about Leoni's gun," Morrow asked.

"Over and done with," the Chief told him.

"The Tiki Bar incident?"

"Let's just say that one has been solved."

"It has," Connolly asked.

The Chief looked up at him somewhat annoyed.

"Do you think no one noticed your car in the parking lot that night? Or any number of our officers from Court that night?"

The Chief turned and looked at Morrow.

"Yours too, with a young lady asleep in the back."

Morrow tried to hide his shock but couldn't. The Chief looked at Big John.

"Yours too, John. The whole thing is over and done with. But that's not why we're here. I got a call today, from Agent Donovan. Anthony Vincelli is being released today. He may have been framed by a rogue F.B.I. Agent."

Fertid sat down on the Chief's typewriter table and held his index finger up.

"Without you guys saying anything about your guilt or innocence, I think we have to act under the mindset that he thinks you killed his son. I'm meeting with the prosecutor to see if we can stop his release but it doesn't look good. In the mean time, you guys need to be on your toes. Vincelli has been inside for a quite a while. He is going to want to flex his muscles. We are heading into dangerous times."

CHAPTER 50

UNDERCOVER HOOKERS

Santee, California

Anita was naked, sitting in the bath tub with her arms around Clay's chest. He was leaning back against her knowing she would not let him slip under the bubbles. Teresa was straddling him and doing all the work as he leaned back and went along for the ride. Hospital scrubs, bras and panties were strewn on the floor. New age music played and a fruity rum drink sat next to the tub within reach of Clay.

Anita looked at the thick scars on Clay's head and at his scarred hand which was missing two fingers. What was left of his legs were of no use, but that was o.k. She would hold him and run her fingers through his hair while Teresa rocked gently back and forth on top of the invalid. The bubble bath sloshed to and fro quietly. They had to be quiet since Clay's mother was in the house. As far as she was concerned they were home health aides giving Clay his biweekly bath and massage. She remembered when they first started coming, his mother was a little concerned but as time went on she could see they were taking good care of him. Clay reached for his drink and sipped it and held it over his shoulder for Anita. She took a sip and could see he was watching her. She smiled at him and took a handful of bubbles and water and poured it on his head and ran her hands from his forehead, over his head to the back of his neck. He put the glass out to Teresa who took a quick sip. He then put it back on the table and relaxed against Anita while Teresa rocked back and forth. The water seemed to be going in the opposite direction as she swayed front to back, the water was simultaneously going back to front.

"You having fun Tiger?"

Clay smiled and Teresa gripped the sides of the tub. Clay broke into a wide grin. He knew what it meant. She began thrusting harder and faster despite the sudsy water leaping and spilling out of the tub.

Anita looked at his Army tattoos, pale white skin, and blood red scars and burns. It was hard to reconcile the handicapped man in the tub with the young stud in the army uniform whose pictures adorned the living room walls. Tall, fit and lean with a confident smile and a full future seemingly ahead of him, he was now content to enjoy himself in a bath tub with his two friends and drinking rum drinks. Anita was at first uncomfortable with the situation. It wasn't his scars or disability. As a prostitute she'd had more than her fair share of men with deformities and catastrophic injuries. As she got to know Clay, she became comfortable with him. She learned that from his brain injury he had been prone to seizures but that they seemed to be further and further apart.

As the music played, Teresa rocked and the water was now slopping all over the floor, she could feel him tense up.

"Almost there big guy," Anita teased and nibbled on his ear from behind. She grabbed him tighter and heard him moan quietly then relax. Teresa smiled and leaned forward and lay on top of him glad to be back in the warm water. She looked at him and saw him smile.

"You can't go to sleep yet," Teresa told him.

"We have to get you in your pajamas and bathrobe," she reminded him.

Anita stroked his hair and whispered in his ear.

"You go ahead and take a quick nap. I have you." She could feel him relax on her as she brushed the bubbles off of his face.

She could hear Teresa rise, the water dripping on Clay.

"Oh my God," Teresa said quietly. "I think he's passed."

Anita placed her index finger on her lips. She stroked Clay's hair and pulled him back.

"Give him a few minutes until we know for sure."

Teresa lay on his chest and put her arms around him.

"There's nothing left for him here anymore except for us and his parents."

As he lay in the water, held by two naked women his smile softened as the warmth of the bath began to fade.

CHAPTER 51

THE END

Richie sat in the motel room replaying his first tryout in his head. He wondered if it could have gone any better. He was too excited to go to sleep so he turned the television on. His phone rang and a familiar voice asked for him, or rather, the new him.

"Mr. Haslett?"

"Yes?"

"How are you making out?"

"Not bad. I had my first tryout today."

"How'd it go?"

"It went very well. I'm back out there tomorrow again but hopefully I can hang in there."

"Good, good," the voice on the other end said then stopped.

"Something wrong?"

"Your parents are fine but I got a message from your mom today. Your buddy Clay passed away."

Richie could feel a lump in his throat. He lowered his voice for fear it would crack.

"How did he go," Richie whispered.

"He went with a smile on his face, the uh, home health aides were there if that's any consolation."

"It is."

"Your mom says you were a good friend to him."

"It went both ways."

"Well, I'll let you go. I just thought you'd want to know."

"Wait, how is Mooj doing?"

"Fine. He's running with our Vegas crew now. He's a good man. He speaks very highly of you."

"He is," Richie agreed.

"Listen, if things don't work out for you in baseball, give me a call. We can always use a experienced people."

"I will, on the half hour."

"I'll let you know what this whole operation is about if you come back."

A sudden pounding on the door interrupted the call. A half dozen would-be professional baseball players were in front of the room.

"Hey numb nuts! Come on! We're going out for dinner.

Put your skirt on and get out here!"

"Gotta go. I appreciate the call."

"Sorry about your friend."

"Me too. Thank you."